Arise, My Darling

By

Amber
Anthony

Credits

Cover by KAM Design

DepositPhotos: konradbak

Bigstock: B-D-S

Editing by Professional Editor Services

Dedication

To every seeker after the mysteries of the Universe. If you wonder whether you can incorporate your understanding into your daily life, you *can*.

"Then worry for nothing, for the Creator is worried for nothing."

References

In this book, we explore the ideas of astral travel and multiple planes of existence. There are many avenues to the study of spirituality. Each seeker has an individual path. The most important element is your intention.

Thanks to

Our Beta Team: Angela S., Ann L., Emily B., Joan S., Katherine B., and Randi B. We cannot write in a vacuum. Your time and insight get us 'here' — bright blessings on each of you every day.

To Rusty's husband Tim, and our supportive friends.

Tuttle Oklahoma, Eighteen Years Ago

Jacob King, age six, held his Grandpa Art's frail hand. Jake was the only family member at his bedside these days. "Gramps, you told me the light would be beautiful. Can you see it?" Gramps' eyes opened for the first time that morning, and he stared enraptured at what he saw.

It was hard for Jake to say goodbye to his Gramps. He watched with sweet pain as the older man's spirit grew younger after it left his tired body. Jake's heart lifted as he watched his grandfather's soul journey into the light.

Grandpa Art, from whom Jake inherited his gifts of sight and knowledge, was the only person in the boy's limited experience who either believed or understood him. Jake's mother grudgingly allowed their relationship to continue because his grandfather held considerable purse strings. The family had a roof over their heads and food in their bellies thanks to Gramps' unconditional love. The old man did not harbor the religious bigotry his daughter and son in law espoused. His reward and Jake's was his relationship with his intuitive grandson.

Jake's parents often piously announced, "Well, we're good followers, but we're poor." Even at his tender age, Jake could see being 'good followers' in their highly dogmatic faith, did not preclude them from taking money from the 'heathen' in their midst.

"Bye, Gramps," Jake whispered tearfully as his parents and their close friends gathered on their knees.

Their pastor piously remarked, "It's a pity the old man wasn't one of us. We tried, but he wouldn't let go of his heathen ways."

A young-again Gramps looked back at Jake just before the beautiful white light enveloped him entirely. "I'll be back to visit, kiddo, don't you fret."

But Jake did fret. He knew Gramps was a good man with the same amount of pride and regret, virtue and evil, love and disdain in him that plagued all mortals. He hated the way the others spoke of him. "Grandpa Art is too going to Heaven!" He insisted, only to gain his father's wrath.

"Don't you contradict your elders, boy." His father admonished, reaching for his belt buckle. "We'll decide who's going to Heaven, not some snot-nosed kid!"

"Aw, Manford," a fellow church member intervened, "let it go. The boy just lost his grandfather."

"He did too go. I saw him go into the light." Jake insisted in a whisper of diminishing volume as he eyed his father who punished him for the slightest provocation.

Manford's face grew red with fury. "I've told you before not to spout that heathen blasphemy around the members of our fold. By God, I'll whip that devil right out of you!"

Jake cried because of the beating of course, but more than anything he cried for the physical loss of the one person he loved.

Thank goodness Gramps was faithful in visiting him after his arrival on the other side. Jake would never have survived his childhood without him.

****

Because Jake could talk with spirit, he spent endless hours in the woods learning from Gramps in the years that followed. In his formative years, Gramps materialized more completely, or perhaps Jake simply had a child's clearer sight.

Gramps took advantage of that clear sight to show Jake how to follow the thread of vibration that told each creature's story. He taught Jake to fly with the hawks. The hawks taught him to focus and see situations from a different and higher perspective. Jake ran with the deer and learned compassion, kindness, and unconditional love.

As Jake mastered reading the forest animals, Gramps explained that people and situations were much the same. "Follow the psychic thread to their core and let the impressions come."

The older Jake became, the less he visibly saw Gramps, even though his perceptions grew consistently more accurate. Before long, Jake perceived a little more than he wanted. He became reluctant to shake hands, afraid of the glimpses into private affairs the contact could engender. Still, his clairvoyance saved him from beatings; he knew when to stay away and when to lie low in his bedroom.

Gramps' frequent visits in spirit left Jake well equipped to leave home for college. He was gifted a small sum of money and property that compounded until his eighteenth birthday. It was enough to buy an old car and pay tuition at Edmond Community College. Jake was finally out from under the thumb of his family and would never look back.

Chapter 1

Las Vegas, Nevada, Present Day

This is the longest shift of my life! Jake King swabbed off the surface of the Thunderbird Casino bar and glanced at his watch which he could have sworn was running backward. Jake was sure there was a drunk and misfit convention in town, and every one of them wound up in his face tonight. He clenched and released his fists, closed his amply lashed onyx eyes in exasperation, and let out a sigh of pure torment. Once already, he'd had to help security escort an unruly customer out. He wanted to get out of here before another of the rowdies pulled a new stunt.

This was not what he imagined work at a Las Vegas strip casino to be. Where was James Bond playing Baccarat? Where were the Bond girls? Jake caught many a worthy woman's eye, and why wouldn't he? He was prime material, or so he'd often been told. He did his time at the gym, sure. The age to build a hard-muscled, lean-hipped body was in his mid-twenties. The bar he serviced, just one of many dotted throughout the casino, sat in the middle of the blackjack tables. One of the blackjack regulars winked at him and gave him a commiserating smile. She'd frequently commented on his "black Irish good looks." Yeah, all that and five bucks would get him a chai latte at Teas Around the World.

Jake wasn't interested in that stuff. He knew good looks were an accident of genetics. Jake had plans. This job and a few windfalls from exercising his gift funded his education.

His inheritance from Gramps had seen him through two years of junior college. He'd worked a part-time job and rented an apartment with a continually changing assortment of roommates. His parents were a real annoyance begging for money. He thought his father might give up and get a steady job, but he never did. So when Gramps' money got low, Jake picked up stakes and moved somewhere his relatives wouldn't look.

He spent a little time at Stanford University in his junior year but was too late to apply for a scholarship. He couldn't afford more than a three-credit class every semester. He met some brilliant people there but also felt dead-ended. Yeah, Stanford was a primo school, but the cost of living was astronomical.

So Jake said goodbye to the temperate weather and rarified atmosphere of Palo Alto. He gave up the proximity to some of the best friends he'd ever known and moved to the much less expensive Las Vegas area where jobs were plentiful, and money always circulated. Jake attended the University of Nevada, Las Vegas as a full-time student in communications. He'd graduate in less than a year. The bar back job at the Thunderbird was just enough to keep body and soul together while he finished.

He caught sight of himself in the mirrored bar, his short and sharp haircut looked a little long and not so sharp. *I need a day off, if only for a trim.* His lean, broad shoulders drooped with fatigue that was more than physical. With Jake's level of sensitivity, the sheer crush of humanity in casinos -- those desperate for a payoff, those on the make, and those resigned to bitter disappointment -- crowded him with their emotions.

A fifty-something convention goer stood at the end of the bar, flushed with a big win and a little high on the rum and cokes that fueled him. He jingled the change in his trouser pocket as if expecting Jake to take his order. "What do you suggest to celebrate a big win?" He challenged.

Jake looked to both sides to be sure he wasn't observed and replied, "A soda and a taxi to the airport."

The man snorted. "I'm upstairs in the penthouse. I've already been comped."

"Milk and cookies? They're really satisfying this time of night."

"Are you sure you work in a casino?"

"You didn't ask me about that. You asked me what I suggested to celebrate a big win. For you, sir, I suggest you go back to Dayton on the first flight possible, pay your daughter's tuition, and tell your wife she can quit her second job."

The winner glared and stalked around the end of the bar where Jake stood stacking glasses. "I don't know who you are or who hired you..." The man caught Jake's wrist and jolted back in surprise, which was the usual reaction. No one touched him in anger without having a disturbing energy current set them back on their heels. The aggressor stammered and glowered.

Jake slipped out of his grasp and laid a gentle palm on the man's shoulder. "Sir, nobody's after you. Your heart is open to me, that's all. It's open to a lot of suggestions right now, good, and bad. The good ones are waiting for you at home."

The winner staggered back. "Huh?"

"Have a good night, sir." Jake folded his towel and left it. Looking down the length of the under-lit bar at the bartender, he said, "Jackie, I'm clockin' out. Take it easy."

****

Jake was almost out of the employee breakroom where the time clock was when Bunker, the casino's bar supervisor, caught him.

"King!" He snapped. "I've had a complaint about you. You told a casino whale to go home to his wife and kid?"

Jake closed his eyes and prayed for patience. "Yeah. He asked me what to do to celebrate a win, and I told him."

"Goddamnit, King! I'm not having this talk with you again!" I've told you before; you leave that psychic crap at home. You don't bring it to work."

"Yes, sir."

"In case you haven't noticed we make our money on fools who win and feed it all back into the machines."

"Yes, sir. I have noticed that…"

"In my time I've seen every kind of superstition from rabbits foots to medals of St. Jude, to evil eyes. There is no such thing as luck or magic!"

"Yes, sir."

"So, why would you tell this guy to go home? Your hoodoo tell you to say that?"

"No, sir. You told me."

Bunker drew himself up indignantly. "I did *not*."

Jake let an ironic smile sneak out. "Yes, sir, you did. I've heard you say it a dozen times, 'the only way to win is not to play'."

"I do say that…" Bunker admitted. "But I don't say it around here. When did you hear me say it?"

"Oh, I don't remember exactly, sir. Just here and there."

Bunker shook his head in disgust. "It's good to know you listen to me, King, but pick the correct time and place. Don't ever say it to a player."

"Yes, sir, I'll remember that." Jake waited for a beat and could practically see Bunker searching his mind for a time he would have uttered his favorite warning in Jake's presence. "Uh, is that all?"

"Yes, that's all. Remember what I said."

"Yes, sir." Jake reiterated. As he walked away, he tried to remember exactly where he *had* heard Bunker give that advice. It could be he'd picked it out of Bunker's mind as he walked through the casino mentally berating the players. *Huh, whaddya know?*

****

Slipping into his road-worn 2005 Mercedes Benz C Class, Jake frowned in annoyance when the heavy metal radio station blasted at him. He dialed it down. "Not tonight." He pushed buttons selectively, letting out a deep breath when the bass line introduced Diana Krall. *You put on a good show last month, Diana, it was worth working a double.* Jake took all the short cuts known to the locals, and the lights of the Las Vegas strip receded in his rear-view mirror.

His apartment off Sahara and Paradise was not far from work. He was often teased that it was an 'old lady's apartment' and he had to admit, in the strictly aesthetic sense, that was true. The average age of the residents was mid to upper eighties, and most had lived in the place at least sixty years. But Jake dug the mid-century vibe of rat-pack wealth and prominence he could read beneath the decay. In its day, this apartment house had been a ring-a-ding pad for all the swingers in town. Frank, Dino, Joey, Peter, and Sammy attended many a radioactive party here.

The door warped with the sprinkles of rain they'd had today, and Jake put a shoulder into it after he unlocked the deadbolt. He sighed. His refuge. It was good to be home.

He kicked off his non-slip oxfords at the door, shrugged out of his black brocade vest and padded to the kitchen for a decaf Arnold Palmer. At midnight he sat in darkness, sipping the cold drink. Ordinarily, he'd flip on The Tonight Show or take a shower, but tonight he had the strong urge to light some candles and meditate. Couldn't hurt to let the Universe re-balance him after the day he'd had. *The truth is, I haven't felt right all week.* Something teetered a millimeter away from his mental grasp.

All week he'd been disturbed by mental glimpses of what he'd come to call 'his' girl on the beach. Her memory haunted him since childhood. She was his ideal woman, a face and form so perfect that, even in Vegas where beautiful women gathered by the droves, he'd never met anyone to rival his girl on the beach. In his soul, he felt their connection. Her kindness soothed him; her joy roused him. She was the ying to his yang, and her absence was unbearable.

Jake stared into the candle flame as his mind wandered to a preteen memory. He was twelve and just starting to appreciate the fairer sex. Gretchen McAllister in his homeroom class definitely had his imagination in high gear. She fired many a young man's hormones with her blossoming figure.

Jake liked Gretchen alright, but she couldn't compare to the woman he saw in his dreams. The girl on the beach. Jake took that problem straight to Gramps in the spirit world.

"How old are you in these dreams?" Gramps asked as Jake walked along, aimlessly peeling bark off a dead limb. "Can you see yourself, or are you inhabiting a body?"

"No, I can't see myself."

Gramps pursed his lips, "Then I think this is a memory."

Jake considered and nodded. "Yeah, I think it is."

"How old is the young lady?"

"She's old; she looks like she's in college. Her shirt's tied up under her you-know-what's and her shorts are barely buttoned. Those shorts are really short." Twelve-year-old Jake grimaced. "We're holding hands and running. I don't know why we're running."

Gramps chuckled. "I guess she's an attractive young lady. Do you think she's your girlfriend? Are you running from danger?"

Jake shook his head. "Not the kind of danger you mean. The kind of danger Mom's always warning me about."

Gramps squelched a laugh. "So you have feelings for this young woman?"

Jake felt his face flush. "When she looks at me, I get all twitchy." He smoothed the front of his blue jeans and shifted from foot to foot. He looked up at his Grandfather. "If this is a memory, do you think this could be a past life?"

Gramps nodded. "We've talked about that; you know you've lived many lives before, and you may choose to live many times again after this life. What happens after you and she run on the beach? Does the dream go on?"

"It gets kind of fuzzy after that. I see us going back to, like, a big beach towel and she's kinda straightening herself. You know, tucking in her shirt and buttoning her shorts and I'm… putting on a shirt. Her hair is really long and blowing in the breeze. She's thanking me for her love beads." Jake threw up his hands. "Gramps, what are love beads?"

"Love beads were just another name for necklaces in the 1960s."

Jake shook his head. "She keeps telling me to go to Canada, that I don't have to report for the draft?"

"You know, many young men in those days went to Vietnam. Do you have this memory a lot?"

"I get flashes of it more and more now. But it's always the two of us on the beach. We were in love. I loved her so much, Gramps."

"Souls who love each other often reincarnate with the intention of finding each other again."

"Yeah, but how will I know it's her?"

"You'll just know…"

Jake drew himself out of the memory and began his usual meditation induction, asking the Universe for protection and clarity. Mentally, he walked down a staircase of stones nestled into a forested hillside. The steps led to the edge of a tranquil pond, which he rarely reached. Jake was almost always deep into his meditative state, his consciousness far away from the confines of time and space when he reached the half-way point

Chapter 2

When his foot fell on the tenth step, Jake stood before a bright blue door covered with cartoon figures. He opened it and found himself on a sidewalk outside a row of shops bordering a series of swimming pools. He walked along, admiring the sunbathers in colorful bathing suits, a perfectly blue sky, and white sand surrounding artfully laid-out cabanas.

Before long, he felt drawn to an ice cream parlor with pacific blue siding and crisp white wood trim. Double doors led into a world of comforting confections. For him, the hues of the jars of candy and photos of comfort foods was a playland. Children giggled and squealed as overflowing silver dishes of ice cream treats were set before them.

What a wonderful childhood they must have. Jake envied them the pleasure. His parents had been too absorbed in their strict religious beliefs to allow such pleasantry. They would have looked at the cartoon characters and cheerfully costumed staff as 'demonic'. *When I have children, I'll bring them to a place like this.*

Jake wove between the tables of happy families, absorbing the feelings of joy. A welcoming young man waited at the counter as he approached. The man straightened the black bowtie topping his starched white shirt and blue striped apron. He greeted Jake with a friendly, "What'll it be, Jake?"

"What's good here?"

The bell on the door rang, and everyone stopped to look at the young woman entering. She stunned them into silence with her natural beauty as she stepped through the door in a one-piece bathing suit the color of the sun. She removed her dark glasses and hung them in the neck of her hot pink lace cover-up. Flashing an enchanting smile to the room, she took a deep breath. Gleefully, she hugged herself, and her lips moved in silent appreciation. Her full, long lashes shaded violet eyes alive with the anticipation of pleasure. She unloosed a clip in her upswept tresses, and a wealth of golden-brown hair framed her happy face.

Jake stopped breathing. *She's the girl on the beach.* He remembered running his hands through her flowing hair. *It was silky and warm and smelled like plumeria.* His heart soared, and his words stalled at his back teeth. He gasped in a breath. All he could do was smile.

Taking a seat next to Jake at the counter, she smiled politely at him and greeted the server. *Doesn't she know me?* The lingering scents of lily, cinnamon, and myrrh bewitched him.

Another memory of another lifetime when the two of them were together flooded his awareness. For a nano-second, he had a vision of Egypt before recorded history, when the Nile valley was a verdant subtropical paradise. He was less than ten years old and walked hand in hand with a young girl. They skipped in and out between columns of a pink granite temple. As he watched, the image of the young girl superimposed itself over the woman next to him.

"Hey, Barney!" Her cheerful voice called Jake back to the present. "I'm dying for a root beer float!"

Jake couldn't help grinning at her. "You recommend it?"

"Barney makes the best ever."

Jake tried to concentrate, tried to look normal in this extraordinary situation. His eyes searched her face instead of the menu, and he looked up at Barney. "Make one for me, too, please." Jake stole another look at the girl and looked back at Barney. "How about a double veggie burger with grilled onions and mushrooms?"

The girl smacked the counter. "Grilled onions! Oh! I love when they get caramelized. So good on burgers." She nodded at Jake. "I love to run my fries through that buttery goodness. Barney, make me some fries with a side of grilled onions, please?"

Barney nodded over his shoulder. "Comin' right up, Cricket!"

Jake heard her name, but another echoed in his mind.

"Nofret," a gentle maternal voice called, "come at once. You and Merkha are tardy for prayers!" He knew the woman before him was the child, Nofret, and he had been Merkha.

They'd been raised together in the temple of Nut, married, and lived within temple walls along the banks of the Nile. That lifetime was long and satisfying. They spent happy hours with their children, grandchildren, and great-grandchildren, serving the people of Dendera.

Again, Jake was called back to the present and found his tongue to begin a conversation. "Cricket. What a great name! What's Cricket short for?" She blushed, bringing roses to her peaches and cream complexion, but didn't answer. After a beat, he went on. "My name's Jake." He looked around. "I've never been here before."

"Really? I come here all the time."

He studied her and began to realize the other patrons were holographic. Their actions looped every fifteen to thirty seconds. *But she's as real as I am. Why doesn't she recognize me?* "Now that I know this place is here, I'll have to come again. So, Cricket, why did you draw me here?"

"Don't be silly. I don't even know you." She tossed her hair back over her shoulder in a way Jake found enchantingly familiar.

"Don't you?"

"Don't I what?"

"Isn't there anything about me that seems familiar?"

She blushed. "I'm so sorry. *Should* I know you? When did we meet?"

Their food arrived. "We met a long time ago. It's okay if you don't remember me." They ate in a companionable silence usually reserved for old friends, but Jake could almost see her searching her memory, trying to place him. He watched the movements and chatter from the crowd become more mechanical as time went on.

She leaned back into the support of the bar chair and patted her stomach. "I'm stuffed with such good feelings."

He took in her slender figure and lithe, tanned legs. "Are you a ballerina?"

She covered her mouth with a giggle. "Maybe once…" She sighed sadly.

He decided against pursuing the subject. Jake pushed his empty plate back and spun the barstool around to face the customers. "So, no kidding, Cricket, why did you call me here?"

He read the confusion on her face. "Me? I didn't call you…"

He beamed and took her hand, which she gave willingly. "You come here all the time. I've never been here before. You know we're the only *living* souls here, right? This is a place you've created. Maybe from memory?"

"We often vacationed here when I was a little girl."

"Someplace you feel safe?"

"Of course." She leaned back and gazed into his eyes.

Jake persisted. "Are you in a place you don't feel safe in the physical world?"

"Why would you ask me that?" Her voice grew flat.

Jake watched the atmosphere morph as they spoke. The colors dulled to a uniform grey. The windows grew bars, and the sunny day turned pitch black. Jake gestured to the darkening atmosphere. "I believe there's something you aren't telling me." Her classically beautiful features saddened, and she looked away. "Do you wanna get out of here?" He offered his hand as he jumped from the barstool.

"Out of here?"

"Let's take a walk."

Cricket took his hand and slid from the seat. Their footsteps echoed in the empty cavernous room. Back on the walkway, the sun pleasurably warmed his tanned skin in a friendlier way than the dry Nevada heat.

Jake caught her elbow as they walked. "Cricket, are you in danger? I find people often call me when they're in danger."

She studied his face. "Why is that?"

"Oh," he heaved a sigh, "I was bullied a lot as a kid."

"From your classmates?"

"No, my father. He used to belt me around a lot. At seventeen I put a stop to that, and I guess in a way I've been fighting bullies ever since."

"I see." She nodded sagely but offered no more information.

"So, is someone in your life bullying you?"

"I don't know if he's really a bully. I mean, he just sees me differently than I see myself. He would never physically hurt me."

"But his words are hurtful?"

"Oh, we're making too much of this. Thanks for coming to visit me here, Jake, or…" She gestured around, "Wherever this is. It's very nice of you to be concerned. I have to be going now."

"But…" Jake palmed his face with both hands, to absorb the import of her admission, shielding his ebony eyes from the sun high in the sky. When he dropped his hands, she was gone. The white fluffy clouds with light grey bellies that earlier brought a smile to his face faded. He didn't know this place, but he needed to. He needed to find her again.

He was puzzled as to why he would recognize her, but she didn't know him. There was no doubt in his mind they had been mates in that Egyptian lifetime. But more importantly, *she* was *the girl on the beach.*

Chapter 3

Ordinarily Jake spent Sunday morning in bed after such a grueling week, but the meditation about Cricket the night before disturbed any rest. He put on his hiking clothes, packed a lunch, and set off for Mount Charleston for the day. At least at an elevation of ten thousand feet, the weather was about twenty degrees cooler than the Las Vegas valley. The outdoors was his church.

****

Jake hiked into his favorite overlook spot on the mountain. All he could think about was his strange encounter with Cricket. They'd definitely been together in Egypt, but most importantly, *she was the girl on the beach!*

"Gramps, you there?" Jake opened his canteen and took a long swallow. He noticed Gramps rarely materialized now, but he could always feel his presence and hear his voice.

"What's on your mind, son?"

"I met the girl on the beach. There's a problem…"

****

The shadows on the mountain moved a few degrees by the time Jake finished his explanation.

"And you think she called to you because she needs help?" Jake heard Gramps' concern in his voice.

"She was elusive about that, but it's the sense I got. And there's more… I'm not sure what plane she's on. We met on the astral plane. She hasn't crossed over, I'm clear on that, but she's not really…"

"Could she be ill, perhaps dying?"

Jake nodded and sighed. "I've asked myself that. If she's dying, what can I do to help her?"

Gramps paused. "I've greeted many friends as they've crossed over. They have their spiritual guides, masters, and loved ones close around them at that time. There's very little help needed unless it's a soul who's afraid to die."

Jake picked at the cuticle on his thumb with his index finger. "I didn't read that from her at all. She's visiting places she enjoys. She flirted with me until I asked if she was in danger."

Gramps sighed, "Could she be in a coma?"

Jake's eyes widened. "I didn't think of that."

"Maybe her abuse is more emotional than physical? Maybe she needs someone to bolster her sense of self?" Gramps prodded.

"Oh yeah, I would agree with that, definitely. But I feel there's more to it… this guy may not be physically threatening her, but could she be vulnerable in some way and he's taking advantage of her?"

"This could have been a random meeting. You may not see her again. For people as sensitive as you are, Jake, there's constant chatter between our worlds."

"I'm not saying you're wrong, but Gramps, she's *the girl on the beach.* I had a distinct memory of us together in Egypt, too."

"Well, the next few days should tell the story. But remember, your young lady has angels, masters, guides and loved ones around her all the time, just like you do. This burden is not on your shoulders."

Jake's tone was glum. "It sure feels that way." Jake felt a spiritual hug from Gramps, and he held on tight to keep that feeling. "But, she's supposed to be mine. Why doesn't she know me?"

"Son, her perceptions might not be as sharp as yours right now. We've said before that your sensitivity helps you remember past lives others forget. You've spent your lifetime meeting her on the beach. But the truth is, people aren't meant to remember past life details."

Jake hung his head and ran a hand through his hair. "She's normal, and I'm the freak."

"She's probably a little more sensitive now. If she's spending time in the ice cream parlor, she's lingering longer than most on the astral plane."

Jake perked up. "You think if we keep meeting on the astral, she might recognize me? How do I find her again?"

Gramps flashed images of the hawk and deer to Jake's receptive mind. "Just like you followed the vibration of the hawk and the deer, you can follow her vibration. If it's meant for the two of you to meet again, you will."

Chapter 4

San Francisco, California

Asher Parks enjoyed brunch at the Pier Market on San Francisco's Pier 39. He found the food acceptable to his aristocratic tastes and watching the sea lions sun on the rocks was always a delight. It also afforded him the opportunity to stroll, wearing his wolfish smile while he posed at several tourist photo spots. He was a peacock in his designer clothing.

Asher stood taller when a young woman's gaze locked on him for more than a few seconds. Behind the reflective lenses of his oversized sunglasses, and under the brim of his stylish Bidwell hat, Asher gazed back, his lips reverting to his usual know-it-all grin.

His impeccable style turned heads, and he gloried in that. Little did the public know his bespoke fashions were made to his careful specifications. Parks imported specially woven linings that protected him from electronic probes, particularly government probes. Then there were the always vital hats. He had an extensive collection and was never without one. His assortment included a variety of fedoras, Bidwells, wool Kangol 504s, and the ever-popular baseball caps, each one lined with extremely thin sheets of lead in the crown.

Asher never shared these peculiar safeguards with others. He'd tried before, right after his appendectomy at the age of seventeen. He'd told his parents about the brain implant the doctors inserted during surgery, but his parents became alarmed and notified the school counselor who suggested a psychiatrist.

What a flipping waste that was. None of them were smart enough to understand. After a few family sessions, Asher decided he was wiser to keep his mouth shut. He was a master at playing the 'normal' game.

His seventeenth year was a year of many firsts. Asher had a growth spurt and puberty exploded his world. Tormenting thoughts of missing his glorious destiny warred with his knowledge that the government wanted to silence him.

His father's invention of a new catalytic something-or-other made oil refining slightly eco-friendlier, and that shot the Parks' from the world of genteel poverty to the heady heights of the nouveau riche.

That may have been when Asher began hating his parents. He felt they wanted to keep the riches to themselves. They both got new Mercedes, and what did they get for Asher? Asher got a high mileage sub-compact Chevy that could barely make it up the San Francisco hills. How insufferably embarrassing was that?

His father had gone through MIT on scholarship and felt Asher should work for a scholarship as well. Stanford had been Asher's dream, but he had neither the grades nor the test scores. Again, his father was too cheap to make a simple donation to ensure admission. He got stuck with Cal State at Chico. The ultimate humiliation.

So his parents wanted him to make it on his own? Yeah, he'd do that the old-fashioned way. He'd marry money. That was his plan, and that was what he did. Now that he was a member of the one percent, he often felt as if he lived in two worlds. There was the world of the 'oblivious' those people with so much money they didn't carry cash or think about anything but their pleasure, and the world of the 'hostiles' – who were out to get him.

Today, dressed in his carefully constructed, though stylish hat and clothes, he was safe to make his monthly journey. On the first Sunday of every month, it was his ritual to dine at the Pier Market before hopping on his Sea Ray 350 coupe sports boat for a trip to Gable Island to visit his comatose wife.

He was far too young and attractive, in his mind, to live with such a burden. On the other hand, it got him plenty of attention from women who also found him too young and handsome to be removed from the market in such a tragic way. Not that he was removed from the market now that Constance was – as she was. He had the protection of being married, but there was none of the inconvenience of cheating on a real wife. His dates not only didn't blame him for 'cheating', but they also pampered and soothed him through the experience.

This farce of marriage would come to an end soon. Well, as soon as the court battle settled. As much as he consoled himself with 'just a little longer', attorneys had a way of dragging things on interminably. When they finally did come to a settlement, and the automaker forked over the fifteen to twenty-five million for Constance's 'care', the care would become unnecessary. Constance could then conveniently shuffle off this mortal coil.

After brunch, Asher ambled to his boat. It was a good hour's journey under bridges and past coastlines to arrive at the tiny secluded island where Constance, her staff of full-time nurses, and the island caretaker resided. He could have housed her anywhere. Full time in a nursing home would have been a good deal less expensive, but the caregivers would also have been nosier. He wanted complete control over Constance, and foreign caregivers on Gable Island ensured there would be no debate.

****

The Sea Ray rocked gently against the dock, as Nico, the Brazilian caretaker, moored the boat. The Portuguese-speaking staff was exclusively Brazilian, and Asher owned them as his LLC owned the island.

Less than an acre across, the land was as forbidding as Asher Parks himself. He detested the climb of the steep staircase from the dock to the garden; however, it reinforced the island's hostile geography and discouraged sightseers.

Luana, the head nurse of the staff, greeted him deferentially as he came through the door. "Mr. Parks, I believe we have good news for you this month."

"Good news?"

"Yes, sir, we've seen some increasing signs of consciousness in Mrs. Parks. At times, she seems to be tracking us with her eyes."

Asher snorted. "I thought you were an experienced nurse. You must know these false signs of consciousness occur all the time in comatose patients. The physicians have been quite adamant that Mrs. Parks will never regain her senses."

"But, sir…"

"Tell me what's really important. Have you maintained her turning and massage schedule?"

"Yes, sir. Her skin is pristine."

"Is she tolerating the tube feedings? No chest congestion? No vomiting?"

"No, sir, in fact, we feel she may be trying to suck on the sponges when we clean her teeth."

He scoffed again. "Instinctual. It means nothing."

She tucked her chin at the reprimand. "Yes, sir."

"Doctor Baptiste has increased her vitamin drops. One full dropper for each bag of feeding formula." He handed a sixty-milliliter glass bottle stoppered with a dropper, to the nurse.

"Yes, sir, that's quite an increase from half a dropper. Were there deficiencies in her blood work?"

Asher shrugged indifferently. "He didn't say." Pulling several envelopes from his jacket pocket, Asher taunted, "I have your cash for the month." Her eyes lit up. "Remember, you are my guests on this island, when you leave here I will return you to Brazil. Your being here was never an immigration opportunity."

"Yes, sir. Do you wish to see Mrs. Parks?"

He nodded. "As long as I'm here…"Asher stared dispassionately at the shell of his wife. Her once radiant golden-brown hair now trimmed in what would generously be called a pixie cut, thin and patchy from wear on the pillow. Her once carefully manicured nails were hidden in padded mittens to keep her from scratching herself or pulling out medical tubing. The nurses fought contractures by passive exercises three times a day, though they warned him, at some point even that would be a losing battle.

"Look, Constance, your husband, has come to visit!" Luana declared cheerfully, earning her a scowl from her employer. She didn't say another word.

Asher's glance took in his once stunning young wife from head to toe, and that was it. He turned on his heel and left the room, never seeing the blink and then opening of her violet eyes, with the spark of life behind them.

Chapter 5

Las Vegas, Nevada

Jake worked a double the evening before when the relief barback called in sick. The look Jackie gave him was too pitiful to leave unanswered. He was dead on his feet. He'd had precious little sleep the day before, and after sixteen hours on his feet, he was ready for a refreshing swim to stay awake on the drive home.

He changed into the board shorts he kept in his employee locker, added a tee-shirt, and set off for the elaborate hotel pool. He whistled past the in-pool bar, waving at Howie, the hunky, muscled bartender who nodded a greeting. Afraid he'd doze off if he sat for any time in the chaise, Jake dropped his towel, kicked off his shoes and headed for the deep end. He posed as if to dive in, and immediately heard the lifeguard's whistle.

"C'mon Jake. It's hard enough keeping the tourists straight. You know there's no diving."

Jake looked around. "Aw, Eddie, there's no one here to see…"

The guy gestured to the cameras. "I'm here to see, so be a good boy and just cannon ball."

Jake entered into the still, cool water. It would heat up considerably in the next few hours, which made seven AM the right time to swim. Jake did a few laps and shaking his raven hair out of his eyes, saw a few bathing beauties had the same notion.

Three girls twittered together like starlings until they saw him emerging from the steps, wiping the water sluicing off his muscular chest and arms. He felt admiration in their excited whispers. *Good. I worked hard at the gym to get this way. I'm glad somebody appreciates it.* "Good morning, ladies! The water's great!"

"Yeah, I love this pool!" One bold blonde co-ed answered. "We're from Mississippi. Where're you from?"

"I live right here in Vegas. I have a membership at the hotel spa."

"Really? Then you must know all the hot places. Maybe you could be our escort?"

He toweled off and shrugged. "I know where not to go."

"That sounds like the place for us."

"You heard me say *not* to go, right?"

She pouted prettily. "But we want an unforgettable adventure. Won't you show us a good time?"

Jake sighed. "Why don't you come over here. I'll read your palms and tell you what kind of adventure you're going to have."

"Oooh!" The redhead scampered to him. "I love palm reading and all that stuff."

"Yeah?" Jake pulled out a chair for her at an umbrella table and took a seat himself. He took her hand perfunctorily, barely glancing at it. "So, you like this guy you're dating?"

She glanced around at her friends. "Well, yes…"

"Then I'm guessing you don't want to screw it up by getting arrested, right?"

"I can't get arrested. I'm in law school."

"Yeah, that would kinda put a crimp in becoming the first congresswoman in Mississippi."

Her eyes glowed. "Congresswoman?"

He grinned. "If you're smart, and stay out of trouble, yeah, Congresswoman. But maybe that can't compete with an 'unforgettable adventure'."

The brunette with Jackie-O sunglasses and a huge straw hat marched over with an air verging on contempt. She pulled the sunglasses down her nose and gave him a skeptical look. "This guy's a con man. Don't listen to a thing he says. What's next, you'll give us winning KENO numbers for a price?"

"Oh, Michelle, you've been such a bitch this whole trip." The blonde sniped.

Jake sat back in his webbed chair and gave her an appraising look. He glanced at the other women. "Would you ladies give us a minute alone?"

The redhead hedged. "I don't know…you're not mad at what she said are you?"

He chuckled. "I get that all the time."

Michelle waved a dismissive hand. "He wouldn't dare touch me." The others reluctantly stepped into the pool.

Jake gestured her into a chair. He slid his sunglasses down and fastened a stare at her, visualizing the ugly scene with her boyfriend in his mind's eye. He knew the reason she'd been irritable during their vacation. "You had a horrid argument with Lenny before he left for summer break."

She sniffed. "That douche."

"I agree. So why do you bother with him at this point? He's already said he won't help you."

"He has his qualities."

"I think your family will help you. Yeah, they'll be unhappy with the news at first. It'll be a shock…"

She leaned in and whispered, "What do you mean? What news?"

"The baby. They'd rather see their little girl happily married, but that's not going to happen with Lenny. Your folks will love your baby as much as they love you, and given a little time, you'll meet a good man, and you'll be a happy family."

Michelle stood abruptly, stumbling over her heavy iron chair in the process. She regained her footing. "You're disgusting!"

"Excuse me?" Jake rubbed at the beginning of a sunburn on his nose. "I thought you would see this as good news. Look, you've been in a bad mood since you got here." Jake stood and righted her chair as she hovered uncertainly. "You can't sleep. You're not drinking." He placed the padded cushion back in the chair and motioned her into it. "Your friends don't understand, and they're giving you a bunch of crap for it." Jake retook his seat and tapped his forefinger on the table for emphasis. "If you go home, tell your family what's going on and make plans, all that stress will evaporate. You're going to have a beautiful little girl. She'll be the best thing that's ever happened to you."

"You can't know any of this." She sagged back into the chair, subdued.

Jake studied her face before he spoke, hoping to avoid more drama. "Tell me I'm wrong."

She watched him for a beat, and then fat tears cascaded down her cheeks. "You think it's possible? My parents are very conservative. My father always said he'd disown me if I came home pregnant."

Jake lowered his head and looked up at her through his lashes. "When you're a parent, you'll amaze yourself. Your child will be your priority, not your prejudices. Believe me, I know about religious bigots, but your dad will be your knight in shining armor. They'll all come around, and I'm telling you, your family will be in love with this little girl, and they will be there for you every step of the way." He held an open palm out to her. "Your father is going to offer you a position in his company, and you're going to change the way he does business."

Her friends, seeing her distress as they emerged from the pool, ran to her side looking daggers at Jake. "Shelly, are you okay?" The blonde comforted. "What did he say to you?"

"Don't be mad at him. It was nothing bad. He touched my heart, that's all…"

"Aw…" The redhead sighed. "Did he convince you to go for it and have some fun?"

"Em…more like, he convinced me to head home and take care of business." Looking up at Jake, she announced. "I think we should rent a car, drive home, and stop at some nice places along the way, like the Grand Canyon and Sedona…"

"The Grand Canyon?" The blonde whined.

Jake stood and clapped his hands together. "The Grand Canyon! You'll love it! Beautiful spot!" He made a namaste gesture and strode off without another word.

****

That afternoon, Jake's nap was fitful. He expected an active dreamlife, but this sleep was more like a disjointed nightmare. He saw Cricket with a man, his features indistinct, but as Jake read him, he knew the stranger had murder in his heart. Cricket

33

and the man argued, she pointed at what must have been a costly set of golf clubs and then hurried for a red sports convertible. She revved the engine, clicked into her seat belt, and peeled out of the driveway with a grinding of gears. The guy holding the golf bag, Jake guessed was a lover…a husband… watched her go with great satisfaction. The hair on the back of his neck stood up. *This will not end well.*

She drove swiftly down a steep and winding canyon. Her wheels squealed in protest, but she put the car through its paces. She rounded one severe hairpin turn, and her right rear wheel skidded off the road into a pothole. A mind-numbing crack of metal shook the air, the car went one direction, and she went the other. The abrupt stop, which should have been mitigated by the seatbelt, sent her airborne despite the restraint.

Catapulted out of the convertible, Cricket smashed onto the unforgiving pavement. Jake prayed she didn't feel the impact and the scrape of the road. Behind her, the car burst into flame. Oncoming motorists skidded to a halt, cell phones in hand, making frantic 911 calls. Someone covered her with a blanket. Another checked her pulse.

Jake awoke trembling in a cold sweat. *Is she still alive?*

Chapter 6

It had been suggested to Jake more than once that he could make a lucrative living giving psychic readings and working as a medium. That was not where his interests lay. He knew he'd eventually work to promote spiritual concepts, meditation, universal philosophy, and healing. He saw himself more as a teacher than a reader.

His friend Des, however, had a respectable amount of psychic talent, and Jake knew him to be honorable as well as ambitious. Obviously, the Universe knew it too, because Des was given his chance much sooner than he'd expected.

"Jake, geez, last night blew my mind. DeBlasio threw me on stage. I didn't have a choice. But when the spotlight hit me, it was like lightning."

Jake leaned back on the barstool and chuckled. "Des, you've got enough P.T. Barnum in you to camp it up. You were born to be on stage." He waved his hand, demonstrating a marquee. "Desmond the Magnificent, Mind-Reader to the Stars!"

Jake and Desmond met in a consciousness studies class at the university. They were heavily involved in the class study group. It was an academic way to explore psychic phenomena. Jake was by far the most gifted and experienced psychic in the group. Desmond had what he described as 'flashes of knowing' since childhood, but he hadn't had a Grandpa Art to guide his gift.

They bonded over their boring jobs as casino barbacks and traded stories of on-the-job psychic hits. The game they developed to train and hone their gifts quickly expanded their accuracy and confidence. Each spent time during a shift, secretly reading patrons and assessing the skill of their predictions — the game built Desmond's confidence. Jake escalated to speaking his prognostications aloud as he had with the big winner a few nights ago.

Before long, word got around their social circles. Jake was grateful no one at his casino was anxious to throw him on stage. He gave Desmond a sympathetic grin. "So Milo the All-Knowing showed up drunk, and DeBlasio just shoved you on?"

Desmond gulped air. "Pretty much. I was so terrified my mind kinda shut down, and something else took over."

Jake jabbed him with an elbow. "C'mon! You loved it."

Desmond shook his head low over his iced tea. "No, dude, it's not like that. Those strangers sitting in the dark -- their energies are on steroids. They arrive at a mentalist show ready to have their minds blown. They all want proof of something supernatural. The hardest thing for me, was all those spirits sending me symbols all at once, and I'm trying to figure out who belongs to what symbol."

Jake snatched up two bags of chips and offered one to Des. "I can see the problem. What did you do?"

Des shook his head 'no' to the chips. "I asked my guides to organize the spirit crowd for me and spoon feed it to me."

"How did that work out?"

"Surprisingly well. I was accurate about eighty percent of the time. But then, the freakiest thing happened…"

Jake sat forward and nodded. Des looked profoundly uncomfortable. "Well, don't keep me in suspense, man, what happened?"

"A woman, in the back of the room, kind of in shadows… hard for me to see…"

"Yeah."

"I guess she kinda went into a trance. I'm sure it wasn't conscious unless it was the creepiest practical joke ever. I mean, you wouldn't pull a joke like that on me, would you?"

Jake watched his friend, mystified. "Ya got me! On a night I didn't know you were working, doing a job I didn't know you'd be doing, I pranked you."

Des wouldn't let it go. "Well, you could have planted a practical joker for Milo, you could have meant it for him. You always said he was a fake anyway."

Jake gave his friend a level look. "No. I did not plant a shill in the audience for you or anyone else. What happened that got you so spooked?"

Des squirmed, looked away, and rubbed the back of his neck. "There was a couple I followed out. I had to give them a private message, kinda ominous…" Jake nodded. "The kicker is, when I walked back onto the dark stage, there was a woman, alone in the audience."

Jake shrugged, "Did she want a private reading?"

"Uh, no. This woman went into a trance. This awful voice came out of her, not a woman's voice at all. Old Testament,

Biblical…" he shuddered. "I mean, like a monster voice…" Jake raised a brow. "It said, 'The savior must act quickly. Evil forces align against her. Tell him.'."

Jake gawked. "Tell whom? And who was she talking about?"

Des frowned, opened his mouth to reply, and suddenly a voice, not his own, boomed through the room. "The danger of the water is isolation. The danger of earth is the distance. The danger of air is its absence. The danger of fire is the destruction of evidence."

Jake leapt to his feet. "Who are you?"

There was no answer, just Des shaking his head in disorientation. "Dude, is that a trick question?"

Jake looked around wildly. "You didn't hear that voice that came out of you?"

Des rocked back. "No. But I felt like, a power surge. Like there was too much energy in me."

Jake nodded vigorously. "No joke! I don't know who this entity is, but he's cryptic, and he's powerful. I sure as hell hope he's on my side!"

Des' tone was sober. "These messages are for you, aren't they?"

Jake frowned. "I think so."

Des continued. "Reading a room full of curious strangers is a snap compared to what you're mixed up in. What *are* you mixed up in?"

Jake rubbed at his forehead and considered. "Have you ever done lucid dreaming?"

Des paused. "I've had vivid dreams. Dreams where I know I'm astral traveling. Isn't that kind of lucid?"

"Now that you say that, you're right, it is astral…"

Des took a long draw on his tea and scratched at the back of his neck. "So, what's going on?"

****

Jake felt pleasantly exhausted and relieved of his obsession with the mysterious Cricket after his martial arts class. There was nothing like the mental discipline and physical exertion of Brazilian Ju-Jitsu to make you forget your troubles. He took a quick shower and changed. Still wiping errant drops of water from his hair, he headed toward his car, his sweaty gi under one arm.

Inevitably, his phone rang at the most inconvenient moment. He fished his cell out of his pocket, hoping they were not calling him into work early today. "This is Jake King."

"Hello, your majesty! This is your loyal subject, Lady Sandra." A female voice chirped.

Jake cocked a brow and grinned. "You have leave to speak, Lady Sandra. You are appropriately curtseying, I assume?"

"Indeed, Sire. Lord Paul has bid me, 'get his ass down here for a round table'."

"You know I have a job. I can't just leave whenever I want." Jake put the phone on speaker and laid it on his car's roof while he unlocked the door and threw in the gym bag. He put the phone back to his ear and leaned against the car in the shade. "I have to give two weeks notice on a vacation request. When is the tournament? I have a particular set of skills that are hard to replace here."

"Slow your roll, your Highness. It's the third weekend of next month, in celebration of our Haight Ashbury opening."

Jake gave a low whistle. "Haight Ashbury! What'd you do, rob a bank?"

"Nope. Aunt Lindsey died and left us a gorgeous painted lady. It's zoned commercial, so we figured, what the hell, we'll have classes in the storefront and live above the shop. Hopefully, we can afford the property taxes."

"Well, I'm sorry to hear about Aunt Lindsey, but that's great. I'll put in the paperwork today and see you in July. At least, it'll be cooler in San Francisco."

"You have a standing offer to stay here with us, you know. We need another trainer. Paul says you're great with the old ladies."

Jake smirked. "Sure. You say that now, but when I'm on the cover of AARP with my silver-haired gang, you'll eat those words."

"Remember, San Francisco City College has free tuition. I'm just saying, work here, live with us, finish school…"

Jake turned serious. He and Sandy had been an item a couple of years ago, though they wisely decided they'd be better off as friends. "Oh, I'm pretty settled here. But I'd love a little vacation in San Fran."

Chapter 7

His laptop was ancient, but it surfed the web well enough. *How do I find a woman named Cricket? That can't be her real name.* Jake settled with a large glass of spring water and fed the name into a missing person website. After two hours of searching every kind of site he could imagine, he was down to googling women twenty to thirty, pet names. He got book titles, names of dogs, names of cats, and children's nicknames, no beautiful young women in danger. In frustration, he closed the lid with a small thump.

Jake settled in his meditation chair. He was too edgy to walk down the stairs to his tranquil pond. Today, it was more jumping from one cloud to another. He fell on the last one and spiraled ass over tea kettle, landing on a dirt road that led to a white building with a rough pine door. He turned the knob and walked into an English pub. The swinging sign above the door read The White Horse. He looked around. Somehow he knew *she* was expecting him. Cricket waved to him from a substantial wooden booth hidden in a nook away from the more sociable patrons. He grinned and crossed to her.

He appreciated the emphasis of her slim curves in the russet-colored jodhpurs and high-topped riding boots she wore. Her shirt was snowy white with a cravat at the neck, and her luxurious hair was pulled back in a tidy chignon. Jake thought she looked delicious in a one-part librarian, one-part pillow fantasy way.

She gestured at the laden table as she approached him. Before he could react, she embraced him enthusiastically and kissed his cheek. Instead of hay and leather and horses, he caught the throat-closing odor of hospital tubing and antiseptic.

"Oh, I'm so glad you came!" Her breath was stale and metallic. The feel of her body against his was disturbingly light and brittle as if his gentle hug could break her bones. She certainly didn't feel like the healthy, vibrant woman she projected. He prickled with goose flesh and strained to hold on to his frozen smile.

Her cheerful voice continued as if looks meant everything. "I didn't want to dig into all of this by myself." Jake glanced down and saw their meal was replete with every traditional English dish he could name. He struggled to join into the fun of her fantasy.

He knew she projected the way she wanted to be seen; perhaps how she had once been? At the same time, it was apparent she was in grave health. He fought to look unperturbed as flashes of the accident he'd witnessed in his dream played in his head.

Jake cleared his throat. "Looks almost as delicious as you do." The radiant smile she sent him broke his heart.

"Would you like a beer? I sweet-talked them into chilling the glasses."

"I'm usually not a drinker, but I'll have what you're having."

She smoothed the hair twisted at the nape of her neck. "You'll love this; it's an ale. You like fish and chips or a Sunday roast dinner?"

"You really love to eat, don't you?"

Cricket lowered her voice to a conspiratorial whisper. "I don't get to do it very often. So, when I get a chance…"

Jake sat back, his hand over his heavy heart and watched her savor the flavors. "You know, I tried looking you up today."

She put down her fork. "Looking me up? How?"

"Online. I couldn't find anything about a girl named Cricket. Is that your given name, or maybe it's a nickname?"

"You have to try these mashie peas! They are to die for," she continued gaily. "Were you going to ask me on a date?" She winked at him, and he felt her foot tap his.

Jake sampled a spoonful of peas. "You bet! If I could find you, I'd ask you out. So, how did you get the name Cricket?"

"I don't remember. Some things are kind of fuzzy. When we used to come here, we'd get off the plane, and this would be our first stop. It's close to Heathrow, you know. Daddy would say, C'mon Cricket! Time for lunch."

He tried another tack. "You're dressed for riding. Are you going after you eat?"

"You didn't see my horse outside? Did he slip his lead?" She rose in a panic, and he caught her hand.

"It's okay; I didn't see a horse because I came through the back."

She placed a hand over her heart. "Oh, thank God, I thought Prince had broken loose."

"C'mon, sit down and finish your feast. Prince is fine, and I'd miss you if you left."

Her smile dimpled at him. "Well, we can't have that. Wouldn't you like to come riding with me? Do you like horses?"

"If they like me."

She scrunched up her nose. "Spoken like a man who doesn't know horses."

"Ya got me." He paused, uncertain of how to broach the subject. "You remember the last time we met?"

"At the Boardwalk Ice Creamery, sure."

"Every spare moment I have, I think of you."

"You do? Well, I've been dreaming of you, too."

"I was worried, though, because you said you might be in danger, and then all of a sudden, you left."

Cricket's expression grew grim, and she laid down her knife and fork with a clatter. "Why would you say that?" She looked away from him, head bowed. "I was having such a good time."

His hand covered hers gently. "I don't want to spoil our good time, but I'm concerned. You said you were in danger."

"Did I say that? I don't think I said that."

"You did."

Their conversation was abruptly interrupted by hurled pottery. It skittered on the wood floor near their feet.

A young woman deep in shadows smacked her hand on the table, her question shrill. "Why did you need more money? You have an allowance…"

The man with the sinister demeanor tossed up a hand casually. Anyone watching them could see he was far from indifferent. "I needed walking-around cash."

"Ten thousand dollars' worth?"

"These are your friends I'm entertaining. Catalina, the boat parties, golf at the club, it's not cheap."

"*My* friends," she scoffed. "How can you call that collection of spoiled trust-fund babies, my friends?"

He grabbed her by the wrists and jerked her forward. "Who else do I meet at your charity events? Just because you're lady bountiful, does it mean we all have to be? You know those charity cases you toil for suffer enough; you don't have to suffer for them."

She jerked her arms away from his grasp. "I expect you to donate the ten thousand dollars you conned out of my banker. You and your friends will have to live more frugally this month."

A wide, open-handed slap across her face punctuated the woman's last statement.

"No!" Cricket's head fell into her hands. Within the space of a blink, she disappeared, and the pub dissolved into static. Reluctantly, Jake opened his eyes and heard Mrs. Matsky's over-loud television. The poor woman was deaf as a post.

Chapter 8

Marin County, California

In the dark, the view of Belvedere Cove from Corinthian Island was mesmerizing. A few scores of boats bobbed across the cove at the San Francisco Yacht Club. Their lights flickered like dragonflies and held Asher's attention.

Absentmindedly, he stretched his legs out on the deck lounge chair. His wife's five-story waterfront home would do for now. For some damn reason, she adored these tall houses standing like sailors along a bow. Asher would have preferred someplace secluded, where he could see approaching guests before they parked and knocked on his door. Here on Corinthian Island the house was awash in bright sunlight and bombarded with the sounds of the bay and exuberant neighbors. It required Asher's constant vigilance.

Today, another letter arrived, forestalling the settlement on his lawsuit with the automaker. It was their faulty seatbelts that left Constance in this condition, after all. If it hadn't been for them, she would have died mercifully in a fiery crash. It was only fair that they pay for her suffering and his too.

Now, there would be even more trips to Gable Island when he'd anticipated eliminating Constance for good. He'd have to endure more sessions with that grief therapist who seemed to discern things about him he'd rather she not know. He glowered; he'd have to make more trips to see Dr. Baptiste in St. Martin. Asher hated to fly.

He ran a dismissive hand over his jaw, dispensing the feeling of a gnat or a stray hair. *I don't like something crawling on me.* He narrowed his eyes, and just to be sure, slipped a Panama fedora on his head.

Tonight he sought the peace of knowing he wouldn't have to go back to Gable Island for another thirty or so days. When the lawsuit eventually settled, it would be so easy to douse the wooden buildings with kerosene and flick a match like a villain in a horror film. The only thing left would be the white brick lighthouse. Nature would reclaim the island within years. It was the circle of… life.

His phone trilled on the deck table. *Jimmy.* If he didn't pick it up, his cousin would blow up his phone like a thirteen-year-old girl. "Jimmy, not tonight." Asher started to close the call.

"Ash, c'mon man, especially tonight. Why are you sitting up there in the dark?"

"Because nosy bastards like you sit across the bay watching me." He glanced up at the stars wondering who else might be watching.

"You weren't there today. Uncle Roger emptied a bottle of Johnny Walker Blue while he was on his tirade."

Asher shook his head. "Rog does that whenever he gets a hair up for it. Don't put it on me."

"You should have been there, man. They presented the family with ceremonial copies of the law, and the Governor gave out Montblanc pens…"

Asher clenched his jaw. "And for every dead parent, you get a pen." There was silence on the line.

"No, I think it's just for every two dead parents. Nobody got two pens." Jimmy snarked. "But why weren't you there? The law was such a big deal to you when you started this uproar."

Asher generated the appropriate emotion. "It's aggravating to see those smug marine engineers standing there looking persecuted when their carelessness killed my parents. Dad loved that yacht. I had to get rid of it. Too many ghosts."

"I heard two of the engineers talking after the service; they maintain they don't know how those live wires got in the water."

"See! They're still covering, and you ask why I don't want to be there? Do me a favor, Jimmy, put away your binoculars for the night. I don't need company; I need peace."

"I don't want you to be alone tonight."

"I appreciate the sentiment. I'm fine." Asher closed that call and dialed his broker. *This idiot doesn't have a life.* "Joe, it's Ash. Since you're making so damn much money off my portfolio, how about celebrating my three years with you? Take me to Danka's for lunch tomorrow around two-thirty."

Joe's reply was a dry, "Two-thirty?"

"Yeah. And wear a sport coat. This is a nice restaurant." Ash closed the call and turned off his phone.

Chapter 9

Las Vegas, Nevada

Jake brewed Des a stronger black tea. "She never answers direct questions."

"Like what?" Des crossed his one leg over a knee and leaned back in the easy chair.

"Simple stuff. Her name…if she's in danger…"

"Why would you think she's in danger?"

"The first time we met in the astral, I had a sense that she was in danger. I asked her, and she hinted that a man was abusing her emotionally."

Des was equivocal. "Well…"

"And then I had a dream about her. Not a meditation. In the dream, she was in a catastrophic auto accident…"

"So…could she be one of those people left unable to move or speak?"

Jake nodded slowly. "Looking at the accident I saw, yeah, that's possible." He rubbed at his brow. "She says she doesn't get to eat very often…"

Des sat forward. "Is she being fed intravenously, or through a tube? I mean…"

Jake's eyes searched his ceiling without an answer. "That's possible. I mean, they can't feed someone in a coma any other way, right? If they truly weren't feeding her, she'd be dead, so… But, here's the deal, before she got in the car, she was fighting with this guy…he had a husband vibe… and in the dream, I knew he wanted her dead."

Des rubbed at his third eye as if it ached. "So, if you were a woman trapped inside your own body, whose husband wanted you dead, what would you want to do?"

"I'd want to get the hell away."

"Right, but you can't physically get away, so…"

"You put yourself in an altered state to get away?"

Des thumped a fist on this thigh. "Right. And to where do you escape? Places that made you happy in the past." He stopped and pondered. "But that doesn't fit with the fight you witnessed in the pub. Since she creates everything in this altered state, what was she telling you with the fight?"

Jake continued to rub at his forehead just between his eyes. "Well, the couple fighting was in shadow. Who were they?"

"Her parents?"

Jake answered slowly. "I don't think so. Maybe her and the guy?

Des pursued it. "You could hear the voices?" Jake nodded. "Were they the voices from your dream?"

In his excitement, Jake rose and paced. "You're right! They were the voices from the dream. That means it was Cricket and whoever this guy is…"

Des pursued further. "So what did you find out about that couple in the pub?"

Jake frowned in concentration. "She's positively loaded. I don't know if they're married, but I suspect they are, and he's going through her money like water."

"That's a powerful motive for murder." Des bit his lip.

"Yeah."

"Do you think you could describe her to a sketch artist? I have a friend downtown who does these incredible pastels. Maybe she could get a good approximation of her looks since we don't know her name. It would be a step in the right direction. You could put it on the web, you know, 'HAVE YOU SEEN THIS WOMAN'."

"God, that's a wonderful idea! Yeah!" Jake grabbed up his keys. "Let's go."

Des ambled to the door. "Yeah, if you've got some cash, it'll probably take a while, and she doesn't work for free."

Jake clapped him on the back. "For this, I've got all the money we need. In fact, I'm gonna hit the out of town casinos tomorrow. I need a war chest."

"No kidding? You are actually attached to her…"

****

The Marie Antoinette Resort and Casino in Primm did not meet the standards Jake came to expect from the Strip. No active smoke filters, so he might as well have lit up a carton himself. The sounds of the place echoed deafeningly. Jake resigned himself to a late breakfast at the buffet while he waited for the golf tournament to end.

53

He'd bet ten thousand at the Sports Book on Roy McAvoy to win the Open Championship in Kent, England. Nothing was ever a sure thing, of course, but he did see McAvoy defy the odds to win and hoist the Claret Jug over his head. The odds would give him a tidy payout. He'd never laid down such a large bet, large bets drew attention, but this situation demanded it.

All Jake knew, and he knew it with his whole heart, was he had loved Cricket through lifetimes, and she was in mortal danger now. He had to find her; he had to get her away from that husband. Hopefully, Jake could help her heal.

He ambled around the buffet, trying to work up an appetite. The scrambled eggs took on a dark yellow, plasticine appearance. Jake swallowed hard and turned to the deli section, where there was yellow cheese. He could make a cheese sandwich with an English Muffin. There were a good selection of juices, but all the ice surrounding them melted. He wondered if he took a banana and a cup of strawberries to the bar, would they blend it for him? *Oh, this will do, I've eaten worse in my life.*

The bartender, for a five-dollar tip, was accommodating about making a smoothie, and Jake sipped it while waiting for McAvoy to be declared the winner. A sudden-death playoff between his guy and a Scottish upstart had him sweating a little, but McAvoy came through in the clinch, and Jake was fifty thousand dollars richer.

That kind of payoff was a big deal at this truck stop casino. The Shift Manager, Sports Book Manager, and Pit Bosses all came over to have a look at the big winner. When it was revealed to be a twenty-four-year-old 'kid', Jake could almost see them consider how he could have played them on the wire. Finding no evidence of a con, after about an hour, they were forced to issue him a cashier's check. He could have stayed overnight at their five-story concrete block building overlooking the solar farm, but he decided discretion was the better part of valor and headed for Mesquite.

The drive was uneventful if incredibly dull. *Talk about one long straight road of desolate desert.* Jake was glad he had the emotional victory of fifty thousand dollars to keep him awake. As he drove, he strove to remember other lifetimes that involved Cricket, but nothing came up. He supposed that was just as well. It wouldn't do for him to fade into another lifetime while driving.

Something niggled at the edge of his consciousness, telling him one person winning too much at once could be dangerous. He needed to be aware of his surroundings at all times and use his green scapular to hide the well-folded check.

His aunt, who was disturbed by his mother's cultish behavior, was a devout Catholic who'd given him the scapular during a visit shortly before he graduated high school. She told him he'd be under the protection of the Immaculate Heart of Mary, and the Blessed Mother would always guide him.

The green scapular was a cloth necklace worn under clothing. It dropped down over his heart in front and back. It was a religious image in a small plastic pocket. When Jake began his gambling trips, he split the pouch and slipped his folded winnings check between the front and back images. *Blessed Mother, I'd sure appreciate you working overtime in Nevada.*

Jake rolled into Mesquite just after noon and decided to explore the new vegetarian restaurant advertised on a billboard. He was pleasantly surprised at their selection and headed full and happy to the hotel/casino to check-in and rest before tonight's adventures in gambling.

When he got to his well-appointed room, he decided to shower and then sat down to see if he could meditate himself out of a sense of agitation. When was the last time he'd meditated and not had Cricket's burden at the forefront of his mind?

Chapter 10

Mesquite, Nevada

Jake's induction began as usual, but this time with a focus on his breathing rather than walking down a flight of stairs. Within what seemed like seconds, he became aware he was on a beach.

He looked back and saw people walking with their swim fins under their arms as they trudged between formations of large, volcanic rocks. Others were sunbathing under umbrellas, some in the direct sun. People pulled on their rash guard shirts and led reticent swimmers with encouraging words. Even outside in this dome of sunshine and fluffy blue clouds, he felt claustrophobic among the crowd.

Adjusting his snorkel gear, he dove to swim to deeper waters where there were fewer people and more fish. In amusement, he spent quite a while watching a purple crab guard his rocky home.

He was caught off guard by brightly painted fingernails waving before his mask. The hand fluttered in front of his face.

It was Cricket… grinning broadly. They popped up, treading water in the depths.

"What are you doing here?" She grinned in delight.

"Well, ya know, living in Las Vegas, I never miss a chance to submerge in the cool waters of the ocean. Where do you live?"

She dropped back down and swam toward an arm of rocks that circled Shark Cove. Jake gave chase. They came out of the water to sun on the rocky peninsula. She pulled off her mask and dug in her drybag. "Look! I brought brownies! You don't mind nuts, do ya? People say I'm a little nutty."

"You are a little nutty, but also very beautiful!" He pushed a few dripping curls behind her ear. "Everything about you is just naturally beautiful." He gave her his most charming smile.

"Oh, you're too kind. Besides, have you looked in the mirror lately?"

"I'm glad you like what you see. I was hoping to spend more time with you. We keep popping up in the most interesting places. It seems like you wanna keep me around."

"I'd be a fool not to keep someone around who thinks I'm beautiful! Besides, I love the way you make me feel." She looked away shyly. "I want to tell you something, but I'm afraid you'll think I'm nuttier than ever."

Jake laughed. "I think this whole situation is kinda nutty. What is it?"

"Have you ever had a memory, kinda like déjà vu?"

"Yes." He nodded encouragement. "Go on."

"Do you like San Francisco?"

"It's a beautiful city." His heart rate sped. "Where are you heading with this, Cricket?"

She squirmed on the rock, reluctant to meet his gaze. "Do you believe there could be such a thing as past lives?"

He took her hand and kissed her palm. "I believe in a lot of things, Cricket. I'm not going to judge you. Tell me what you saw…"

She took a deep breath and plunged into her story. "I've had these memory flashes of us together in San Francisco. I think it was in the 1960s. You know, flower children and all that?"

"So we were flower children? Is that what you saw?"

Cricket nodded. "We were maybe eighteen years old? And we were running on the beach. We didn't want the day to end…we were…" She blushed furiously.

"We were…" He encouraged.

"We were in love. We didn't have a nickel to our names. I guess nobody in our crowd did. You were getting ready to go into the Army. You'd been drafted, and we had this big discussion about whether you should go to Canada…"

Jake ran his fingers through the refreshing water. "Running away doesn't sound much like me."

"No. You were going to the induction center, and a few of us were going with you. We were on a cable car in San Francisco, and there was a terrible accident. Over forty people were hurt, but you and I were two of three people killed."

Jake gazed far into the distance, sharing her memory, it all made sense now. "Wow! That was a dramatic exit."

"Yeah." Her voice was sad. "I guess that was a pretty short lifetime." She waited for a beat. "You don't have any inkling about that? Am I nuts?"

"I've dreamed those moments many times. When I was kid visions of you just about drove me crazy. I kept looking for you to appear in my world. I remember us being together in Egypt, too. Do you have any memories of Egypt?"

"I love Egypt! I've always loved their history, always felt at home with the idea of being there. I keep seeing a pink temple."

Jake gazed into her questioning eyes. "I think the essence here is that we've been together before. Perhaps in many lifetimes. Which is why we found each other again now."

"It's peculiar that I think of you, and you appear. Why is that? Nobody else does that."

Jake frowned. "Well, I seem to have this quirky ability. Some people call it psychic or sensitive. I have the ability to travel out of my body. Everyone does. People often astral travel when they dream. The difference is, I can do it just meditating."

"So am I dreaming this?"

"I'm not quite sure. You're in an altered state, that's certain." He hugged an arm around her shoulders. "I think we should just enjoy being together without over-analyzing it." He munched the last of his brownie and refused when she offered him the last one in the bag. "You have it. I love to watch you enjoy your food."

"You know, maybe I just will. If it's rude of me, you'll forgive me, won't you?"

He flashed his most winning smile while she enjoyed the treat. Covering her full mouth, she spoke, "You have the most mesmerizing eyes. Has anyone ever told you that?"

"Now and then. People seem to like the color."

She nodded thoughtfully as she chewed. "That's it. Their depth just draws me in. Can you see into my soul?"

"If you want me to…"

She popped the last of the brownie in her mouth. "That would be nice, but the brownie's all gone, let's look for turtles."

"So soon? Please, Cricket, let's chat awhile."

Cricket tossed the drybag over her shoulder and dove into the clear depths.

Jake shook his head and prepared to follow. He heard the drone of a jet ski and people yelling at the interloper. Pandemonium erupted with every person on dry land.

****

Cricket held her breath and swam low hovering over more red crabs dueling over a safe refuge. Jake saw the disturbance of the jet ski above her. With ferocious speed, he dove to her, grabbed her ankle, and yanked her back toward safety as the jet ski dipped with its turn toward open seas.

Cricket fought the unseen grasp on her ankle, kicking and swinging her arms and free leg. Their gazes met, and Jake motioned up. Recognizing the peril, with determined fervor, Cricket clung to Jake as he headed toward the rocks.

"I didn't mean to scare you; I didn't want you to get hurt."

There within his arms, she was real and slippery and warm. Her hands caressed his face and lowered his mask. She pushed her mask down and smiled with an air of anticipation.

"Thank you, Jake. That was close. I appreciate your efforts to save me."

Jake laughed at himself. "You know, we're in the astral, nothing can really hurt us here. I guess that was an instinctive reaction. I'll always want to save you, darlin'." He watched her blush and blink the crystalline drops of water from her eyes. His voice grew deep. "Is there anything I can do to save you in the physical world?" He asked, solemnly.

She placed an impromptu kiss on his unprepared lips. Dumbstruck, he stared at her. Her gentle palm caressed the side of his face, and she leaned in for another kiss — longer, this time, and with more feeling.

A simple close-mouthed kiss filled him with such elated satisfaction he felt as if he could fly. With a saucy grin and kick of her flippers, Cricket dove into the aqua ocean and was gone. All that was left was his boyish grin.

Chapter 11

Jake opened his eyes in his hotel room. *Might as well get on with it.* He brushed his teeth and shaved to shake off his strangely elated mood. He needed to focus.

It was mid-week, and the casino was slow except for the die-hard locals. A girl group, the Busted Headlights, did their best Tina Turner cover show. Jake wandered through the aisles, dropping coins occasionally in slots, playing a hand or two of Twenty-One. Mostly, intentionally losing, so when it came time to win he'd look like he earned it.

A down-on-her-luck woman in a tired-looking sheath asked, "Do you want a date?" He politely declined but handed her two dollars and suggested she play the machine on the end of the back row in three minutes. She gave him an odd look and stared at the money for a beat.

"I'm serious. Do it." Jake encouraged.

While he shuffled between the aisles, time passed, and the designated machine went off like a Roman candle. The lady on the scooter with the oxygen tank let out her loudest scream as the progressive slot clanged, and the number climbed to twenty-eight thousand dollars. The woman in the sheath watched from the bar, sipping the dollar beer, frowning. Jake saw her motion to the bartender and nod in his direction.

There was another hour to kill before Jake could head over to the Big Bertha machine. It was extremely rare for this machine to hit huge numbers, but a payout of around fifty thousand dollars would do nicely. He played Bertha, putting in a good two thousand dollars before she hit. There were screams of disbelief and excitement. Jake did his best to look appropriately astonished and delighted. The casino brass appeared next to him within seconds along with security, and the bells and lights continued to announce the winner until security turned off the alarms.

The supervisor of the slots area was congenial if reserved. "Did you bring your I.D. tonight, sir? Are you over twenty-one?"

Jake laughed. "By a couple of years. I have my Nevada driver's license right here."

Still genial, the Supervisor inspected his license. "You're from Las Vegas. What are you doing in sleepy Mesquite?"

"Just passing through on my way to St. George."

"Passing through, huh? Guess this is your lucky night."

"It really is! Now I can stick around and enjoy the pool and HBO in the room."

"Uh-huh. Will you follow me, please, sir? If everything checks out with your I.D., we'll issue a check for your winnings."

"Sure thing."

****

The casino manager hung up the phone and plastered on a thoroughly artificial smile. He handed back Jake's I.D. "Everything checks out just fine. If you'd like to have a drink at the bar, it will be just a few minutes…"

"I'm not a drinker. Do you have a Slurpee machine?"

The casino manager's smile stayed frozen. "No. I'll be right back."

In his room, Jake zipped up his overnight case, tossed it in the Benz and was gone before they knew he'd checked out.

****

In the car, he did mental math. He started with his five-thousand-dollar cash stake, and he now held checks totaling eighty-thousand-dollars after taxes.

His Bluetooth headset rang once and announced, "Call from Jackie."

"Hi, Jackie, what's up?"

Her voice was slightly strained, and Jake immediately picked up her anxiety.

"Hey, I heard you were taking a trip to St. George. I'm visiting my Grandma in Overton, why don't you stop by on your way home? She's got some apple pie for you."

Jake knew this was a ruse. She wasn't calling him with good news. "Sure thing. I'll see you at her house."

Off the highway, Jake took a series of unlit, curving streets. He relied on homes with porchlights over their house numbers to find the little clapboard house by the river. Jackie's Toyota was barely visible in the dark carport. She stood in the shadows waiting for him and was at his side before he unhooked his seatbelt.

"You have to get out of here."

"But you told me to come…"

"Great psychic you are. You go back to Vegas and you'll walk into a necktie party. Who the hell did you cheat, Jake?"

Jake frowned. "I don't cheat."

"Well, the bosses think you do. They were all over the bar tonight. I had to fake Gran being sick to get away to warn you."

Jake extended his hand out to Jackie. "You're a good friend to do this for me. Are you okay? They're not gonna come after you?"

She shrugged, "No. I take time frequently to care for Gran. These guys are pissed, Jake."

"Yeah, I guess I've worn out my casino welcome."

"I wish there was some way I could get your stuff for you. You know they're going to be watching."

"It's okay. I have everything I need. I travel light."

****

Back in his car and on the road, Jake called out to the most dependable person in his life. "Where yah been, Gramps? I really need to talk to you."

"I'm so proud of you, son. You are becoming a compassionate and resourceful man."

Those kudos warmed Jake's heart, but he felt a shoe was about to drop. "Thanks?"

Gramps chuckled. "Don't thank me, you're living up to your potential now."

"Do you know where Cricket is, Gramps?"

"No, Jake. I'm sorry, I don't. You see, I've been doing work of my own, it's taking me in a different direction."

Jake caught the hesitation in his Gramps' voice. "Work of your own? What does that mean?"

"I've decided it's time for me to grow some more too, now that you're handling yourself and your life well."

"So…"

"I'll be reincarnating soon, and there's plenty of preparation work for that as you'll find the next time you make that journey."

"Are you saying we won't be able to talk?"

Gramps' voice was compassionate. "Not for a while, son. I'll be in a period of deep meditation for several months. After that, don't worry, I'll be around."

"But Cricket…"

"Don't you worry," Gramps said, sounding eerily like the day he died. "You're on the right path."

"But I need you."

Jake felt an encompassing warmth and heard a whisper, "You're on the right path."

****

He took the Tonopah exit around three AM He badly needed sleep. He wanted to avoid any casino hotels, so his option was The Mizpah Hotel on Main. Who knew it was declared the most haunted hotel in America? Or so the billboards advertised. What were the odds an intuitive on the run would get a good night's sleep when ghosts prowled the hallways?

Jake sighed as he used his keycard to enter an overwhelmingly crimson room, crimson draperies, settees, pillows, and chairs. He closed his eyes and still saw the bloody color. He spoke out loud to the ghosts in general. "Listen, I need about five hours of sleep. Just to keep you busy, I need information on a girl named Cricket. Either her husband or lover is threatening her. I think he's trying to kill her. She's in a coma, and I can't tell where. Any of you have a pipeline to abused women? Help me out here." An invisible hand pulled back the duvet cover on the bed. "Thanks, very much, I was serious about that five hours."

****

Amused by the thought that he would have a typed report on the bedtable sent by a ghostly hand, Jake rose and showered. *If only that were realistic.* He sighed and directed his thanks into the universe for five undisturbed hours of sleep. Digging in his go bag, he found his one change of clothing and left his room feeling refreshed. He followed the ornate columns and gilt statues of women in the lobby to a wide doorway.

How can I be the only one ready to eat breakfast? From the tin ceiling tiles to the ruby carpet, this was a room filled with hidden stories. He had to give them credit; The Mizpah Hotel stood perfectly restored to its early twentieth century roots. He passed a table for four on the right and slid into the booth near the back. *Probably closer to the kitchen, I won't be a burden on the server.*

A woman, impeccably dressed in an austere server's uniform, with a coffee pot, promptly approached him. She turned over his china cup and filled it without question. The server asked him. "What would you like to eat this fine morning?"

"How are the cook's omelets?" Jake slanted looks toward the silent doorway.

She cocked a hip and smiled, "We make the best Denver omelets in Nevada."

Jake made a face, and she mirrored it. "Don't like Denvers?"

"I don't eat meat, how about cheese, mushrooms, green peppers…"

She nodded in agreement until he got to spinach. "If that's what you want, dear. Toast with that?" And she was gone.

He sat back and closed his eyes with one hand on his coffee cup. When it felt cool enough to drink, he opened his eyes and saw a lovely young lady with flaming auburn hair sitting across from him. He jumped. "I didn't hear you, I'm sorry…"

"How long will you be at the Mizpah?" Her voice was soft, with a Louisiana accent.

Jake raised the cup to his lips; it was the best coffee he'd had in ages, but it wasn't decaf. "I have to head off to San Francisco today."

"That's a lively town. We saw photos of the earthquake in the newspaper. But that's not why you're going there, is it?"

Jake swallowed more coffee and narrowed his gaze at the girl in the embroidered linen blouse. "What earthquake?" *What have I slept through?*

"Why the trembler of 1906, of course!" The swinging door from the kitchen opened, and his server pushed a cart with covered plates. He craned his neck to catch sight of the appliances and cooks. *Toto, I don't think we're in Kansas anymore.* The door closed abruptly, and the server silently placed steaming plates of food in front of each of them. She refreshed his coffee, and he debated talking or eating. "I'm Jake, what's your name?" His words caught her as she took a bite of toast. *Do ghosts eat?*

"You can call me Red." Her left hand played with the sausage curl over her left shoulder.

"I'll bet you know a lot about this place, Red."

"I have been around long enough to know a lot about a lot."

He cut some omelet with the side of his fork, and before he could eat it, he dared her. "You wouldn't be sitting here because I asked for help early this morning, would you?"

She smiled sublimely, "If you don't ask the spirits for help, we can't give help."

"How specific do I have to get?"

"You are looking for a woman who has man problems?"

"Yes, I am."

"She's hurt, you're right."

Jake ate for a beat, considering her statement about asking the spirits for help. Was he expecting too much to have the information dropped into his subconscious? Was he going to have to narrow down his questions?

"Is Cricket on this continent?"

Red cocked her head, and her mouth went straight. Jake noticed an old-world map framed on the red flocked wallpaper. He stood up in a rush and pulled it off the hook. Pointing at the United States, he explained. "This is the continent of North America." His finger traced Canada and the United States. "Can you point to where she is?"

Red's index finger traced the old-style printing to San Francisco. Jake nodded and headed back to the empty wall. "She's near water." She took another bite of toast.

Jake spun on his heel. "The whole damn city is near water." He watched her blanche at his words. "I'm sorry, Red." He rehung the map.

Red raised a brow and giggled. "I have heard worse words out of the mouths of men."

"I doubt myself; I'm not doubting you. I'm wondering if I hear the truth or what I want to hear."

"If you are hearing me say, San Francisco by the water you are correct. I thought that was why you're headed that way."

Jake sighed. "I'm headed that way to stay with friends."

Red held out her hand and closed her eyes. "Your friends are good friends. Would you believe me if I told you, you are called to render her aid?"

"In San Francisco?"

"Yes."

"And I'm not making you up? You're real?"

Red nodded. "As real as a spirit can be."

****

Jake didn't remember finishing his breakfast. Only when he packed his dirty clothes and gathered his toiletries did he realize he was back in his room. Oddly, Jake wasn't hungry. He felt as alert as any man who drank two cups of coffee after a good night's sleep. Walking from window to window in the old hotel room, he admired the sight of the antiques. He watched the bed; would the duvet move back into position by an invisible hand? He left, closing the door behind one of his oddest hotel stays ever.

The hotel clerk accepted his key card. "Did you enjoy your stay with us, sir?"

Jake considered her burgundy polo shirt qualified her as a living mortal. He nodded silently, scrutinizing the people in quiet conversation dotting the settees around him. "Where's your breakfast room?"

The clerk directed him with a flat hand toward the wide wooden doorway. As he left the hotel, he stopped short. The room featured broad-planked wood flooring and wainscoting to brighten beige walls. There were no red velvet booths, and the tables held thirty or forty people. Several folks chattered over a buffet line. He blinked and trotted to his car.

Chapter 12

San Francisco, California

Joan Carroll had been a grief counselor for over ten years, working for the oldest and most established mortuary in San Francisco. For the most part, she enjoyed her work. Taking grieving family members from despair back to emotional health was very satisfying.

Why then, did she not enjoy counseling Asher Parks? He should have been her favorite case. The man was an only child who lost his parents in a boating accident and his wife's parents in a home improvement accident. In every practical sense, he'd lost his wife in an auto accident; she lingered in a permanent vegetative state.

All this happened within the past two years. Joan was at her best when dealing with prickly clients whose anger issues pre-dated multiple losses. But being with Parks for a full session always left her with a bad taste in her mouth.

Her training told her he almost certainly had an underlying psychosis, although he carefully compensated and never shared his delusions. He indeed exhibited distractibility and grandiosity. With any other client, she'd refer to a psychiatrist, but Parks was adamantly opposed to the idea even when she framed the suggestion as a means to antidepressant medication. Since he had no living relatives she knew of, she was stymied. The longer she saw him, the more she worried about what hid beneath his carefully constructed veneer. Every time he left her office, she used her lavender aromatherapy pen to erase the bad juju.

Today's session was no better. "How did you feel when Sam challenged your right to sell?" She asked Asher, thinking of the hundreds of people his sale of Nielson Artificial Intelligence would put out of work.

Asher sniffed arrogantly. "Talk about a shirt-tail relative! What right does he have to decide the fate of a Fortune 100 company?"

"Well, he is a relative of the founder, shirt-tail or not…"

Asher's scorn escalated to an outright snort. "He drives a Volkswagen and vacations at Disneyland."

"Nevertheless, he is a blood relative of the founders, has a degree in software development, and is a licensed attorney. I can appreciate why he feels he has a right to determine the fate of the company, now that Constance is incapacitated."

Asher sniffed again. "Hopefully, the courts will align with my vision."

Joan drew in a deep breath and reached for calm. "Asher, I don't want you to be disappointed if the courts side with him. I don't believe they'll allow you to shut down a significant industry in this town. I know you're hurting. Will selling a company that provides hundreds of jobs erase that pain?"

"It's the market today. If people haven't gotten by now that all work is preordained, they'd better wise up."

Joan cocked her head. "Preordained by whom?" She prodded.

"Did I say, preordained?" Asher hedged. She nodded and watched him rotate his fedora compulsively. "I misspoke. I meant, temporary."

"I see." She smiled pleasantly, and the watchful, guarded look ebbed away from his eyes. "We haven't talked about the circumstances of the Nielson's family deaths. Why don't you tell me what happened?"

"Her mother, Kathy, always wanted to restore an old mansion in the wine country. She'd had her eye on it for decades as it crumbled into ruin and their company grew enormously profitable. I believe Dean, the old man, thought it was folly, but it kept her quiet and out of his way except on weekends, and so he indulged her."

"You mean they were only together on weekends?"

"Yes, he stayed in their home in Santa Clara, close to work, during the week and joined her on the weekends. Lucky sod."

Joan looked at the smiling faces of the family pictures Asher supplied at her request. "Do you have reason to think he wanted to avoid being with his wife on the weekends?"

Asher grimaced. "No, he seemed as eager as she when the weekend came around." He rolled his eyes.

"Is it so hard to imagine they enjoyed working together on the project?"

"I don't spend much time imagining." He thought for a beat, and his demeanor changed in an instant from condescending to tragic. "I suppose no one should have been surprised when they walked into the kitchen, turned on the lights, and the whole place exploded. A gas leak. She'd neglected to have the main valve disconnected, and they both paid with their lives."

"Oh, dear." Joan murmured reflexively.

"Yes, very sad," Asher affirmed, not looking sad in the least. "My wife was a wreck over the whole affair. Like me, she was an only child, and I think women are always much closer to their families. It wasn't long after that when she had her accident. I don't think she ever recovered from the shock of her parents' deaths. She was irritable, absent-minded. Perhaps if she'd been thinking more clearly…" He let his words peter out.

Uh-huh. Joan had to bite her tongue to keep from hurling a taunt. She glanced at her watch. "I see our time is almost up. Perhaps you'd like to book your appointment for next week?"

****

The kitchen stairs at Bobo's led to a floor of offices. The manager's office overlooked the dining room through a bank of one-way mirrors. Joan and her boyfriend, who was the evening manager, enjoyed dinner in his office every Wednesday night.

She was taller than average and climbed the stairs, her long legs taking two at a time, to fall into Brian's arms and erase the memory of Asher Parks. Her chin-length golden hair hung in a stylish bob and accented her pretty face. But her large brown doe eyes were her most prominent feature, and the one she used with great success when empathizing with clients.

Brian gave her a hug and a kiss at the door. "I smell lavender. You've had your appointment with that sociopath..."

"Yes." She groaned. "I swear, the more comfortable he gets around me, the worse he gets. He's like a chameleon. I can truly see him changing colors and altering his persona to match. God, he gives me the creeps."

Brian took her light coat. "He does sound extra-creepy. How could he not notice how gorgeous you look in that dress?"

"You are the perfect antidote for a creep!" She ran her fingers through the hair at the nape of his neck and kissed his cheek. "What delicious dinner does Darin have planned for us?"

"You know it's always a surprise…" The office intercom rang. He smiled at her regretfully. "Give me a sec…" He picked up the receiver and listened. "Darin, you have to stop taking all this so personally. The guy's a jerk. Have any other patrons complained their dinners were cold?" He paused, and Joan could hear indistinct ranting over the handset. "Well see, everyone else thinks it's fine, you think it's fine. He wants an issue to reduce his bill. How many did he eat?" Brian shook his head. "Every one of 'em, right? Oh, he left the smallest one. How predictable." Brian stood erect and took in a deep breath. "Send out a cup of the lobster bisque. Be sure it's steaming and remind the server to say it is scalding hot." He turned to Joan. "This must be the day."

Joan walked to the mirror and looked down. "Which one is he?"

Brian joined her. "That guy in the Hugo Boss bomber jacket with the new assistant D.A. at his side."

Joan gripped his arm tightly. "My God!"

Brian looked at her in surprise. "What is it?"

She grimaced at Asher Parks' back. "Ah, let's just say it's the six degrees of separation thing."

****

Jake drove over the Oakland Bridge a little past seven in the evening. Although the rush hour traffic was letting up, he longed to get to Paul and Sandy's place. He'd thought of little besides Cricket and his ghostly visitation in Tonopah all the way to San Francisco. If ever he doubted himself or his talents, this was the time. How coincidental could it be that circumstances sent him to San Francisco? *Try to work up some faith, will you?* Maybe Paul or Sandy could shed some light.

He paid to park in a long-term lot about four blocks from Paul's school and, gathering his overnight bag and computer, said goodnight to his only other possession, his car.

Jake stood under the outdoor camera at the residence door. Siblings Paul and Sandy were flabbergasted.

"What are *you* doing here?" Paul's understated dry sense of humor played across his words. He looked at his watch. "Aren't you a couple of weeks early?"

Sandy jumped down the step to hug him. "Tell me you're moving here."

****

He poured his story out over dinner and held their rapt attention.

He and Sandy had known each other for almost two years during his time at Stanford. Paul became a buddy soon after. They shared an interest in martial arts and states of consciousness. His friends watched the evolution of his gift and helped him focus and grow within it. It was good to be around people who accepted him for what he was without question.

Paul laid a brotherly hand on his shoulder. "You're welcome here as long as you need. The room on the right, next to the bathroom, is yours. You've got a job if you want one. Tell us how we can help."

Sandy stood, her plate in her hands. "Let's put the dishes to soak and go do a meditation. You need more clarity."

****

The three of them sat in modified lotus positions in the training room. Candles flickered around them while sandalwood incense curled up to heaven. Low-toned gongs sounded in sequence over room speakers. Jake didn't even need an induction to find himself soaring out of his body and into a Caribbean hillside cave.

****

The first sensation he felt was a smooth, bamboo rug beneath his bare feet. He looked at himself and saw linen drawstring pants. He was shirtless and barefoot, the epitome of scruffy chic.

Lanterns glowed on tables that flanked a massive canopy bed hung with gauze. Huge soft pillows and silken linens invited the ultimate relaxation. A table at the end of the bed held cheese, fruit, and wine.

Like a specter, Cricket glided out of the shadows wearing a handkerchief linen caftan that hinted at the treasures beneath the fabric. Her golden-brown hair wafted loosely in thick curls swirling around her shoulders. Transfixed by her beauty, he grinned. "This is my favorite destination yet."

She reached his side and melted against him. "Mmm. Mine too. I thought, since we've been lovers before, we might enjoy getting to know each other *better* again."

"You read my mind!" Jake embraced her and drew in the scent of jasmine and vanilla. She felt warm, tanned, and vital in his arms. A goddess of a woman replaced an unhealthy wraith. "You've never been more beautiful in any lifetime." He nuzzled her neck. *She's learned to project fully the woman she wants to be. Does that mean she's getting better or worse in the physical world?*

She took his hand and led him to the mouth of the cave. "We can see the entire valley from here. See the birds?" Jake was amazed to see flocks of the most colorful parrots he'd ever imagined taking flight below them. A giant python curled its long body around a tree limb far beneath the cave, and Jake could have sworn the reptile winked at him. A waterfall tumbled over rocks to their right. Clouds gathered low across the rainforest. "When the rain comes, it's like a blessed embrace, and we're cozy inside." She murmured.

Jake fingered the neck of her caftan and kissed along the side of her throat. "Cozy in bed?"

Cricket purred under his attentions. "That's my invitation. Will you join me?"

Jake sobered. "All of this is everything I could ever want or dream of," he gestured around them and reached for her hand. Their fingers meshed, he kissed their joining and drew her closer. "I couldn't have a better invitation." She smiled. "It will all be perfect unless you take me into your bed and disappear."

Cricket gasped. "No!"

His face felt stony. "I swear to God, Cricket, I won't lie with you unless you trust me enough to help me find you. I won't sleep with an enigma."

"I can't answer all your questions." She whispered and laid a gentle finger on his lips. "I struggle to recall my physical life." Her eyes grew brilliant with unshed tears. "I promise I won't disappear. I'll tell you what I can."

Jake brightened in her embrace. "That's all I can ask."

She gave him a radiant smile. "Then forget your worries. Taste these incredible fruits. I'll bet you've never seen anything like them before."

Jake stared down at hammered copper plates of sliced and peeled fruit. "I'll have to trust you on these…"

She popped a juicy slice into his mouth and immediately covered his lips with her own. He grinned, his lips against hers as he chewed and swallowed the sweet and tangy treat. "Mmm. I don't know what's tastier, the fruit, or your lips." He gathered her closer. "Let's do a taste test." His kiss was deep, searching, tangling his tongue against hers. He knew she could feel his ardor awaken against her belly. When he let her go, he teased, "I like your taste even better!"

"Me too! I didn't think I could like anything more than food, but you're kindling a whole different hunger, sugar."

His fingers made short work of the zipper of her gown, and he watched the fabric waft to the floor. His gaze started at her colorfully painted toenails and traveled up perfectly carved legs to gracefully curved hips. His hands encircled her slim waist and rose higher to weigh the delightful roundness of her breasts. "You're perfection!" He breathed and felt excitement leap within her.

"You have me at a disadvantage. I want to enjoy the view too." He laughed and made as if to lead her to the cave entrance. "Not that view, silly! Those beachcomber pants are meant to come off with one tug. Let me help you." She tugged at the waist tie, and his pants slithered over his hips to his feet.

Her hand caught his excitement. "You're playing with dynamite, Cricket," he warned with a lusty laugh.

She gave him a saucy glance. "I could stand some fireworks."

"Then why are we standing here?" He swooped her up, and with a blistering kiss, deposited her in the middle of the bed. His hands roamed her body. "You are a dream within a dream." He felt perfectly in sync with her. Every movement, every caress heightened their pleasure and brought unexpected joy. They were one. His strokes in her most secret place sealed their fate, and they danced to love's timeless rhythm.

****

Cricket sprawled against him laughing. "We're never going to stop playing like this in bed, are we?"

Jake grinned down at her, a satisfied man. "As long as we're together, we'll sample every adventure in lovemaking."

"Mmm. I like that!" Cricket cuddled under his arm and threw her leg over his.

"Darlin', if we have any hope of being together in more than stolen moments, you have to help me find you."

She turned huge tearful eyes up to him. "Oh, Jake, the me you find in the real world might be a far cry from what you see today."

He rolled her under him and kissed her soundly. Raising his head, his gaze searched hers. "I swear to you, darlin', my soul searched for yours, and you called mine. However you appear in the real world, our love will remain."

"Don't say I didn't warn you." She sighed as he flipped over on his back again and drew her against his chest. "Ask me what you need to know, and I'll answer as fully as I can."

"Where are you?"

She shook her head. "I don't know. All I see is a bed with bars, and stiff white sheets and blankets."

"Bars like a jail?"

"No, but bars to hold me in. I think… like a hospital?"

Jake sighed. "I expected that. But where?"

"I don't know."

"There are nurses?"

"Yes."

"What language do they speak?"

"I think they speak Spanish… I don't know much Spanish. I took French in school."

Jake rolled into her, flabbergasted. "Spanish? Dear God, are you in a foreign country?"

"I don't know."

"We've met in the U.S., in England, in Hawaii, now wherever this is," he gestured around the cave, "an island." He paused to consider. "We're speaking telepathically, so it could be any language. You could be anywhere. Do you understand when the nurses speak in Spanish?"

"Not very much. They usually don't speak to me. It's as if they think I can't understand, or maybe they think I can't hear them. They mostly talk over me, and I assume they're talking about themselves, but I don't understand it."

Jake nodded. "Do they ever play the radio or television?"

Cricket sat up excitedly. "Yes! The Today Show. They play it every morning during my bath. Unless a foreign country broadcasts it too, I must be in the United States."

Jake breathed a sigh of relief. "That's good, darlin', that's really good!" She smiled up at him. "Think for a minute if you can identify any other sounds."

She frowned. "Like what?"

"Well, you know the sound of the nurses speaking Spanish, the television at times, any other sounds? Birds, ships, trains, cars…"

"Fog horns! I hear fog horns. They go up and down in pitch like there are multiple ships, and sometimes they sound close."

"You're amazing! Yes! Fog horns! Do you think you could be near San Francisco?"

Her smiled evaporated. "I don't know." Her voice sounded flat, and Jake had an inkling for half a second that she didn't want to know, she was afraid to know.

He kissed the top of her head. "Try not to worry, Cricket, I will find you." He kissed her lips lingeringly. "And until I do, we'll meet, just like this, and I'll tell you over and over how much I love you."

Chapter 13

Jake maintained astral projection for over an hour, and Sandy started to worry. She didn't think prolonged projection could hurt him, but she wasn't sure it wouldn't. *What if he stays with Cricket and never comes home? Better safe than sorry.* Sandy sat beside him, took his cold hands in hers, and received not a flicker of recognition in return.

She let her clairvoyance encompass Jake. He was with a woman she could only assume was the elusive Cricket. Jake retreated from the woman's embrace. Sandy watched them, they were triumphantly naked, but at this point, their sadness at parting was a cloak over each of them.

Jake fought their separation, and Sandy read his flagging energy. Left unchecked she feared it could leave Jake abandoned on an untouchable plane. She caught his shoulders in her cupped hands, and sternly called him back. He left the stranger's embrace and fidgeted as if he held a book.

As he came out of his trance, he looked at his empty hands. "I thought I was reading Poe. A Dream Within A Dream." Sandy gazed hard into his unfocused eyes. "Despite all the reality I felt with Cricket, there isn't a way…"

Sandy implored, "Isn't a way to what, Jake?"

He hung his head and whispered in a sad voice. "I cannot grasp her with a tighter clasp."

****

Joan searched the Brew and Burger Bar for Barry Michaels. Barry was a Criminal Investigations Detective for the San Francisco Police. He became a working acquaintance after she successfully helped him through a rough patch when his partner died in the line of duty. Since then, he referred anyone within his circle to her if they suffered from grief issues. Now, she turned to him for professional help.

He'd already snagged a booth in the back before she arrived. She hurried toward him. "Sorry, believe it or not, the streetcar got slowed down by a group of tourists who couldn't seem to get the hang of stepping off."

He laughed easily and spread his arm along the back of the booth. "Good to see you. I ordered you a lite beer. That's what you like, right?"

"A beer tastes like the end of the day! That's perfect." She paused to take in the changes she saw in him since the last time they'd gotten together. His hair was a little longer than regulation, his waistline was a couple of belt holes tighter. There were a few more grey hairs in his mustache. "You're looking good despite that little hiccup with your heart. Still planning to retire at the end of the summer?"

Barry stretched. "Oh, yeah, they have a good thirty years out of me, and I've got a map with scenic bikeways, and a group of

86

people who want to ride. We're going to take weeks at a time to travel."

"I never pegged you for liking motorcycles…"

"No, no. Back road bicycles. It's an adventure."

She laughed and tucked a swoop of chin-length hair behind her ear. "It does sound like an adventure. Before you go, would you like to help me break the law?"

Barry choked on his beer. "What?"

"Yeah." She admitted reluctantly. "You know, grief counselors are bound by HIPPA regulations just like every other medical provider, but Barry, I'm telling you, I'm working with a guy who's a sociopath…"

"Well…there are a lot of sociopaths who aren't criminals…"

Joan nodded agreement. "I know. But this guy, I think it's possible he could be a psychopath. Maybe…" She took a large gulp of her beer. "Maybe even a murderer."

Barry got quiet for a moment, and then his eyes flashed. "Has he threatened you?"

"No. He's trying to con me. I think he wants me as a character witness. I think he's planning to murder his wife."

"You'd better tell me the whole story. You don't mind if I take notes?"

She shook her head.

****

Joan was surprised the telling went so quickly.

Barry studied his notes and pondered. "So, two sets of parents dead within two years – his and hers, and the wife's in a near-fatal auto accident less than a year after her parents died."

"Right."

"Three things we look at in a homicide investigation: motive, opportunity, and means. What's his motive?"

"Money," she emphasized, "and I mean big money. Millions of dollars in each case. I wouldn't be surprised if it's close to a billion in the end."

"Yeah, that would constitute motive." He signaled the waiter for another beer. "How did these folks die?"

"I know her parents died in a home accident. Supposedly a gas main explosion on the house the mother was remodeling. I know it sounds plausible. Will you think I'm crazy if I say my client may have had something to do with it?"

"Why would you think that?"

Joan sighed in exasperation. "I don't know why, exactly. It's a feeling. It's a feeling I get every time I talk to the oily creep. That isn't very helpful, is it?"

Barry gave her an understanding smile. "On the surface, no. But I've been a detective long enough to know those gut feelings frequently pay off. Anything else?"

"He supposedly came for counseling because he was so torn up that his beautiful bride was in an accident which left her in a coma. But here's the deal. He's not grieving. It's all a great show; I'm sure for my benefit. He's pretending to be grief-stricken. With her parents dead, his wife inherited a hugely successful software company in Silicon Valley which he's trying to sell. That sale alone will be hundreds of millions. If they ever settle the court case over the accident, that will be another twenty million added to the pot. Get this; he's pissed because her cousin is trying to save the company."

Barry swirled his beer. "Sounds like you've got a little more than a gut feeling."

She leaned forward and tapped her index finger on the table. "And just last week I saw him at an exclusive restaurant with one of San Francisco's best-known Assistant D.A.s."

"Could be his niece," he countered.

"I hope not. Not the way he was hanging on her." Her tone turned sarcastic. "Tragic really, how grief-stricken he is over his wife."

"Okay." Barry nodded decisively. "Let's break the law. What's this nimrod's name?"

"Asher Parks." She said quietly. "His wife is Constance Nielson Parks."

"Asher Parks," he considered. "That name rings a bell for some reason. How did the senior Parks' die?"

"They died in some kind of boating accident, that's all I know. I do know they didn't give their son more than a subsistence allowance before their deaths. He's complained about that endlessly. After they died, he inherited quite a bit. Again, they had a company worth hundreds of millions."

"Okay, if I'm gonna break the law, I'm gonna drag you in deeper. Very subtly, I want you to find out more about his wife. Protect yourself. Cloak it in grief recovery terms. 'To help you, I need to understand everything you've experienced. Tell me about your wife's needs now… blah, blah, blah.' Can you do that?"

"Of course I can do that. It's my job."

"Thata girl. When do you see him again?"

"His next appointment is tomorrow if he doesn't cancel, which he does a lot because, of course, he's 'grief-stricken'. He doesn't like being on the hot seat."

"Let's meet again day after tomorrow. With luck, you'll have the information we need, and I'll check into what I can find on all the dearly departed and his wife. Where's she hospitalized?"

"I have no idea."

"Let that go for now. We don't want to spook him. I'll see what I can find out from the various medical facilities around here. I'm gonna hope; if we break the law, we're gonna catch ourselves a murderer."

****

Cricket didn't like focusing on her physical reality. She hated the boredom of her situation. It stripped her of her looks, her dignity, and worse, any possible meaning in her life. It was sensory deprivation. Without the blessing of her imagination, she would have gone mad months ago. That was Cricket's 'reality'. Would it always be? Was she doomed to this purgatory of helplessness for a lifetime? Jake was determined to find her, to liberate her, if possible. The least she could do was give him whatever clues she had. And if it turned out, she would be forever confined to a hospital bed? She would beg him to let her die and end her torment.

She was aware of the silver cord that followed her like a shadow on every adventure, and she'd had many journeys that didn't include Jake. She watched as the Persians overwhelmed the Spartans at the battle of Thermopylae. She watched the building of the Taj Mahal in 17th century India. She cheered for Victoria and Albert as their love affair bloomed in 19th century London. All these adventures, and many more she experienced in her astral travels, as well as exciting fantasies she fashioned for herself. She enjoyed flying the most, yes, definitely flying. When she got well again, she was going to take flying lessons the first chance she got.

Cricket realized if she was ever to be united with Jake in the physical world, she had to submit to the tragedy of her physicality. She felt clammy, at once cold and overheated. The uncomfortable buzzing in her ears set off the queasiness in her gut. She floated from the clouds into a sick room. There was a body curled up on a hospital bed. Medicinal salves and ointments lay on an over-bed table. A machine dripped blue-tinted liquid down a long tube and under the sheets, she assumed into the helpless patient's body. She knew the body on the bed was her own, but she could not emotionally connect with the pathetic creature hiding under the covers.

The windows of the sick-room were open, and white cotton curtains billowed back into the room. She turned from the body on the bed, noticed the television mounted on the wall; it was turned off. She moved to the window casing and looked out. All she saw was a barren landscape; no grass, occasional dwarfed trees struggled to grow in the outcropping of craggy rocks. Water surrounded everything.

She'd seen enough. All she could bear. Within moments she found herself sitting on her favorite bench, watching the seabirds compete for fish. The sun dropped into the ocean, and the colors of the sunset were magnificent. She observed a boat motor by, black hull, white wheelhouse, an emblem of some kind on the side, and it was flying the Stars and Stripes. She was in the United States. Jake would be happy to hear that.

Chapter 14

Jake was not happy. His time with Cricket yesterday was sublime, but he couldn't stay on the astral plane all his life and neither could she. Since he wasn't willing to give up his mortal body at this point, he needed to find her in the physical world.

He tried to convince himself the Universe had arranged his arrival in San Francisco. As much as he strained to believe he'd heard the messages clearly, he couldn't get over the fear it was all too convenient.

He sat in the kitchen, sipping an herbal tea with Sandy. "Look, I know Cricket is real. I know our connection is real. But she said herself her nurses speak Spanish."

Sandy munched loudly on a bowl of granola. "She said she heard The Today show."

"Yeah, I know she did, but what if I led her into that? I should have asked if she heard anything and then shut up. What if I led her into a memory of a TV show by asking if she heard the TV? It could happen. What if she's… I don't know…stuck in some banana republic in some dinky little nursing home? What if she's in Tijuana or somewhere really close to the U.S. border where they would get the Today Show?"

"Possible I guess. Have some granola. You need to chew on something else." She poured a bowl for him, and Jake grimaced at it. "I've never seen you so distrustful of your gifts."

Jake sighed heavily and poured almond milk over the cereal. "I don't trust it because I'm essentially reading for myself. I can't be detached from what I want to hear."

Sandy munched loudly. "So, would you feel better if you heard confirmation from another psychic?"

Jake crunched the tasteless nuggets and contemplated the idea. "It would have to be someone accurate. I mean, not some Dionne Warwick psychic, but someone solid."

Sandy's glance flashed up at him. "Well, of course. I have a friend I've studied with at the University of Consciousness. She's written several books on consciousness and the different planes of existence. During the first Iraq war, a bomb hit the embassy, and she went into a coma for a couple of months. She was finally transferred to the U.S. hospital in Germany where she recovered."

"So she's been where Cricket is now?"

Sandy shrugged. "I don't know. But, I think if anyone could give you insight, it would be my friend, Treva Munter. She's kinda been there."

"She's here in town? When can we see her?"

"I'll call right now."

****

Treva Munter was surprisingly down to earth. Though Jake didn't know what he'd been expecting -- *gypsy gowns and a coin belt?* He knew better. It wasn't like he walked around trailing incense and 'Om-ing'. Her home along San Francisco Bay was post-war traditional. She ingeniously covered the walls with mementos from her travels to every exotic corner of the world. The rooms were brightly intriguing, as was the lady herself.

"I'm so pleased you called to visit, Sandy." She greeted them in a soft middle eastern accent. "You must be Jake." She extended a manicured hand. "It sounds as if you've had quite a time. Come in, and let's talk."

Over fragrant green tea and ginger cookies, Jake's tale poured out. She sat him at a beautifully carved replica of the Resolute desk and brought out tarot cards wrapped in silk.

"You read with cards?" Jake asked, suddenly abashed for sounding slightly condescending.

She smiled unperturbed. "I'll tell you a secret…" She leaned toward him. "They're a nice confirmation, but what they really give me is something to do with my hands, they offer me an easy meditative rhythm when I shuffle. You've seen mediums who write or doodle as they read?" Jake nodded. "Same thing."

"Okay." Jake felt ashamed of his arrogance. "I've never used any tools like that."

"You should try it. Helps relieve pressure. Though like you, I can't read effectively for myself or those I'm especially close to." She shuffled the cards. "So give me a moment, dear, and let's see what my guides show me." Jake's heart pounded.

Treva shut her eyes, shuffling the cards as she'd done a million times before. Jake could tell it was an automatic motion. Her eyes moved behind closed lids as if she were dreaming. Jake knew the sensation of seeing pictures in his mind's eye. The rhythmic shuffling of the cards continued, and Jake began to understand what she meant by using them for her meditative rhythm. She was not consulting them at all.

At last, she opened her dark eyes and her lips curled in a teasing smile. "Oh, she's stunning, isn't she? I can see the appeal."

"Yes, she is, or at least she was. I believe she's very ill. Until recently she's not been able to fully project herself as whole and healthy."

"I see." She drew a card. "Yes, the Hanged Man, she is dealing with a physical crisis." She laughed musically. "Though she has been having a splendid time in the astral." She winked. "Especially since she found you."

Jake bit his lip. "But where is she physically? Look, Treva, I'm just gonna say it. I think her husband wants her dead. I think she's in real danger from him."

Treva frowned and drew another card. "Yes, a volatile energy." She picked up a card. "Here he is, The Devil, a sinister force against her. So, where is she physically?" Her hands rhythmically shuffled and re-shuffled the deck, her eyes closed. "She's by water…"

Jake stifled a laugh and hung his head. "So I've been told."

Her voice became more confident. "You were told correctly. You were led to the bay area to be in closer proximity to her."

"You're sure about that? Can you be more specific?"

Treva paused. "Give me a moment." Her open eyes became glassy; it was as if she failed to breathe. After a moment she looked at him. "My guides tell me… this will sound incredible to you." Jake steeled himself. "She's on an island."

He snorted. "What? She's on Alcatraz?"

Treva shook her head. "No. Not Alcatraz. There are many small islands around San Francisco." She laid out some cards, studied them, and looked back at Jake. "A seeker of another kind will be a great help in your search. As unlikely as it seems, find the island, and you will find your love. You must hurry, Jake, the threat is advancing quickly. See here." She tapped a card. The Knight of Swords. "Death is coming suddenly."

"Whose death?" His tone was grim.

She tapped the Devil card, and the one she said represented Cricket, the eight of swords, a woman bound with swords all around her. "These two are locked in a fatal conflict. I cannot say who will survive." She blinked glumly at the cards and Jake felt a chill throughout his body.

****

Jake knew almost nothing about sailing; he'd been out a couple of times. He did remember the city's Marina Yacht Harbor, close to where he'd sailed with a friend. *I might pay a visit there.*

He searched islands on Google Maps and eliminated any publicly owned nature parks or protected areas. Three islands in and around San Francisco Bay remained. The specific restrictions on those islands were a matter of public record.

He doubted the island leased by the Northern California Naturists was housing an invalid. Though he did think nudists must catch a cold out there in the middle of the bay.

Island two was the private lodge of a computer magnate, Richie Cook.

And then there was Gable Island. On what looked like a desolate little rock stood a clapboard house adjoining a white brick lighthouse. An LLC called 'No Minimum' was the owner.

All the islands were designated private property, so he guessed you couldn't just walk up and ring the bell. He was also concerned about actually approaching them. What kind of boat was needed? How skilled did he need to be to pilot a boat to an island in the bay? Would he be shot?

The mid-July temperature hovered around sixty-five degrees. The fog burned off by lunchtime, and this Saturday it was on the verge of sunny. As Jake got out of his Uber ride, he squinted in the haze despite his sunglasses. He walked into the Marina Yacht Harbor and approached the first man he saw on a boat. "Hey, uh, I could use some help…" He announced to the sixty-something man who sat coiling line.

"Yeah?" Barry Michaels looked up from the line. "I could use a million bucks, myself."

Jake laughed. "Don't know that I can help you with that, but you might be able to help me."

"Sure, climb aboard. You're not selling anything are you?" Jake stepped clumsily from the dock into the boat. Barry chuckled. "You don't have your sea legs, I see."

"No, I'm afraid I don't. That's why I need help."

"Okay, what's your story, my friend?" Jake gave him an edited version of the hunt for Cricket. "Does this woman owe you money?"

"No, sir."

"You a jilted lover? She give you the wrong number at a club?"

"No. I don't actually know her."

"Are you a bill collector?"

"No." Jake grew exasperated. "I don't want anything from her. I'm trying to help her. I think she might be injured and in danger."

Barry gave him a frown. "So call the police. They've been known to take care of that kind of thing."

Jake nodded. "Probably what I will do, but I've gotta find her first. What am I gonna tell the police, I'm looking for a woman who might be injured, might be in danger, might be on an island but I don't know where?"

"What's her name?"

"I don't know…"

Barry gave him a hard look. "Is this a joke, or are you crazy?"

"Exactly why I don't want to go to the police yet."

"Oh, I see you are crazy."

Jake grunted. "Probably. Look, there's a lot more to the story…"

Barry grunted back. "Always is."

"I swear to God I don't want anything from her. Let's say she's contacting me, and you wouldn't believe it if I told you how."

Barry studied Jake's earnest face. "I'm probably crazy too, kid, but you've piqued my interest. I can take you to those two islands you've identified. My condition is, my expenses are your expenses, you know, fuel, all that."

"Okay."

"And, I go onto the island with you. It turns out; I'm a police detective. So, I won't allow anything illegal, and if this woman is in danger, I might be able to help."

Jake was on his feet, extending a hand. "Oh, man, I can't tell you how great that is! Tomorrow? Can we go tomorrow?"

Barry gave him a firm shake in return. "I don't see why not. Let's meet at ten tomorrow morning. You bring food and soda." He pulled a card from his pocket. Here's my card, my cell number's on the back. If the Ouija board tells you otherwise or you have an attack of sanity, you call me, okay?"

"Sure thing!" Jake plucked out his card in return. "There's my number on the back. I live above that school. I'll be here, no problem."

Chapter 15

The following day began with a downpour, which did not abate. The low areas, at least those that didn't run into the bay, began to flood. Jake looked out the fogged-up windows. "God damn it! Just when I think I'm on the verge, I get stymied. Why would the Universe bring me this close and then dump me?"

"You don't know the Universe is dumping you!" Sandy protested. "Maybe there's a reason for the delay. You don't understand it right now…" Jake shot her a look of pure misery.

Paul dialed up the lighting. "Uh, I'm sure a call isn't necessary, but you'd better call that guy…"

Jake paced in a tight circle. "He still works full time, so we'll probably have to wait till his next day off."

"Yeah. Whenever he can go, you take off for that island. I'll cover all the classes." Paul offered.

"I'm ready when the universe is ready," Jake affirmed. "I guess I'll make use of this time to investigate the hospitals for the best neurological unit in town. I think I'll research the owners of those islands, too. Let's get as much information on them as we can." He paced. "After that, you wanna do some sparring? I feel like climbing right up the walls. It's either that or swim to an island in the rain. I'll swim and pull a barge with my teeth like Jack LaLane."

Paul laid a hand on his shoulder. "I know, buddy. I'll give you a good work out, and if you have any energy left, you can try your skills on Sandy. She's small, but she's a demon!"

****

Barry hung up the phone. No great surprise the outing was canceled for today. It was raining hard enough to consider building an ark. Nothing to do. Hell, he hated staying inside; it felt like punishment. What had his mother said about rainy days when he was a kid? "You can get a book or a game, or I can give you a broom, and you can clean."

He looked around the house. He really didn't want to clean. *Maybe, I'll look up that guy Joan told me about. Let's do an internet search.*

It turned out; there was a great deal to learn about Asher Parks on the internet. He was an okay student, but a big frat boy at California State University at Chico. *That's a big frog in a little pond.* He squeaked by to graduate in business administration.

He worked for his father directly after graduation, and even with a multimillionaire dad, Parks couldn't make a success of anything, probably because he spent more time playing than working. Eventually, he left the company and lived modestly on interest from his investments and his father's reputation.

He married Constance Nielson three years ago. She was from real wealth; the type acquired in Silicon Valley. Barry flipped through Google photos of Asher, drink in hand, hanging behind his wife. They frequented the charitable events supported by the Nielsons, Save the Children, Save the Animals, Save the Whales. Parks put together several companies that bit the dust almost immediately, but one oddball LLC was still functioning, No Minimum, LLC, *whatever the hell that is.*

There was a considerable to-do when his parents died. According to the news, they were floating on innertubes next to their yacht in the marina when his father attempted to reboard his boat. Once his foot hit the step, and he grasped the railing, he appeared to have a seizure. It's assumed his wife thought he had a heart attack. She reached for him, and they were both electrocuted by faulty dock wiring that had fallen into the water.

Further investigation showed the marina's insurance company paid out a damn fortune. Asher Parks got his attorney to contact his lawmaker buddies, and the California State Legislature enacted the Parks Electrical Safety Law mandating specifications for all marinas.

This makes three highly unusual accidents in two years. Sure, the wife could have lost control of her car. That's the most normal incident, but then the seat belt breaks? Joan's gut feeling could be right on point.

Barry copied off a list of all Parks' real estate holdings, and *what do ya know?* No Minimum, LLC held the title to a private island in the bay. A shiver ran up his spine. He didn't believe in coincidence, not after thirty years as a detective.

He grabbed his cell phone. "Jake? I know it's raining like hell, but I've got some information you and your friends need to see. Can you meet me?" He paused to listen, heard excited murmurs in the background. "Pick out a spot for lunch in Haight Ashbury. I'll come to you."

****

Jake ground the heels of his palms into his eyes and drew in a deep breath. "So where is Constance Parks?" His heart thumped a frantic staccato as his face reddened.

Barry swallowed the last of his coffee and shrugged. "If I were a detective, I'd say, the lady is on that island." He grinned, and his grey, caterpillar eyebrows danced. "Oh wait, I am a detective." He sobered. "From what you three have told me, and you have to admit it's a fantastic tale, I'd say we need to get to that island."

Paul shook his head. "The only problem is, there are 'no trespassing' signs all over the place there."

Sandy bit her lip. "We just call the police and say we believe there's a woman in danger."

Jake negated that plan immediately. "Wouldn't be smart to call in the authorities. For one thing," he nodded at Barry, "you told us Asher Parks owns the island. He's her husband, and unless there's something we don't know, he's her power of attorney. He'd throw us and the police off the island as soon as we landed."

"Right." Barry nodded. "Also, there's a woman I want you to meet. I can't tell you more than that. She'll have to. Through her, I know Parks is very well connected politically."

Sandy raised an eyebrow. "What does that mean?"

Barry scowled. "You've heard of Tabitha Daniels? The new assistant D.A. who made her bones kicking the homeless out of the libraries?"

Sandy sniffed. "Yeah, I've heard of her. What a bitch."

"Well, she's Parks' new squeeze. One word to her and you wouldn't get near your Cricket again. That's why we need to pretend we've got engine problems and ask to tie up there until our tow arrives."

Jake pondered the dilemma. "Wouldn't Parks turn to her in any case? I mean, I can find a way into that house. I can even get to her bedside, but unless we get her off the island, he could move her where we'll never find her." His gaze searched Barry's. "Is this D.A. his only political clout?"

Paul flipped through his phone. "Asher Parks is a douche."

The table eyed him and answered in unison. "Yeah."

Paul held up his phone. "There's a guy on the internet; his blog is 'Just Jonas'. He must have a real hard-on for the guy because he follows Asher Parks around to all his social/charity obligations. He's made his name on posting absurd photos of Parks' expressions at these events. The funniest thing? No one in any of the images ever looks happy to be around Asher Parks."

"So…"

Paul put down the phone. "I had no idea who Asher Parks was until Jonas started this campaign of 'who did Parks piss off this week'? Every week, he's pissing off somebody big. So I can't imagine he has lots of friends in high places."

"Well, my research shows about the same," Barry agreed, "and his LLC doesn't make political contributions, which doesn't make him any more popular."

Barry sat back and arched a comically evil brow. "As a police detective, I'm going to tell you to get an attorney ready to file an emergency protective order the morning we go in. That way you can legally remove Constance from the island and take her to a hospital. If you need a referral, I know some good people. But first, we have to be concerned about A.D.A. Daniels objecting to the order of protection."

Jake fought the need to pace in agitation. "How do we control that?"

Barry gave him a triumphant look. "I did a little snooping. The court for the city and county of San Francisco has all their assistant D.A.'s schedules online. Guess who's scheduled to be at her high school reunion next week?"

Sandy laughed. "Can we possibly be that lucky?"

Paul nodded. "It's called synchronicity, my dear, and this situation has been filled with it."

Jake ran a finger along the chrome edging of the table as he thought. "What about Parks himself? Don't we need him out of the picture?"

Barry pursed his lips. "It would be helpful, not critical, but helpful. The woman I was telling you about, her name is Joan, she might know something about Parks' schedule. He has an appointment with her almost every week."

Paul pulled up Just Jonas on his phone. "According to this, he travels a lot overseeing the 'good deeds' of his wife's foundation work. It looks like he's in St. Martin the last week of every month for oversight on hurricane recovery."

"When does he leave, when does he return?" Jake wanted specifics.

"Usually leaves on Mondays, back on Thursdays."

"Okay," Jake pursued, "And Daniels leaves on…"

Sandy scrolled through Facebook. "Looks like Northeast High in St. Pete started their reunion yesterday, and she'll be gone till a week from Monday. Go Vikings!"

Jake digested the info. "So, Tuesday, two days from now, looks like the ideal time to make our move. We need to find our own attorney, and we need the weather to cooperate." Jake looked at Paul, "What's the forecast on the Bay?"

Paul flipped through his phone, "Another example of universal convergence. Rain ends today, then a ten-day forecast of sunny with only a few days of partly cloudy."

Barry nodded. "I'll be ready, and I'll talk to my buddy at the Coast Guard. Of course, this will all look like a giant cluster fuck if we don't find a comatose woman held captive on that island. So if your Cricket isn't there, I expect you," he pointed at Sandy, "to keel over and look dead."

Jake snorted. "She's there."

Barry handed him a business card. "Here a contact number for Medflight, in case she's got some equipment we can't handle with a stretcher. What hospital?"

"Stanford University Medical Center, don't you think?" Jake looked around the table for support.

"Yes," Sandy affirmed. "They have a beyond state-of-the-art neurology center."

"Okay." Barry nodded. "Make yourself an appointment with the docs you think will be the best and make them aware of the circumstances." Barry grew serious. "You need to find someone – preferably a family member, or at least a close friend, willing to take on Parks in court, to become her power of attorney."

Jake sighed wearily. "I guess I can't do it?"

Barry snorted again. "What are you gonna tell the judge, you're her psychic lover?"

"Good point."

Barry pointed at Joan's card. "You call her. She'll have information about one of Constance's relatives you might find acceptable." He slipped a five-dollar bill under his coffee mug, rose and waved goodbye to their server. "You know how to get a hold of me."

Jake rose and reached to shake his hand. "This throws us into your workweek. Is that a problem?"

Barry smoothed his Tombstone style mustache and smirked. "I'm less than thirty days out from retirement. They aren't going to bust my chops over a day off. Business is slow; everyone's getting along."

Jake tapped Joan's card on his palm and nodded as the table made their goodbyes. "I'll go alone, I don't want her to feel it's a kidnapping."

Paul and Sandy followed Barry out the door as Jake thumbed Joan's phone number and pressed 'call'. Her number rang with the odd droning buzz of an out of work line. Jake sat back down and leaned his chin on his palm, watching the rainbows in the street puddles outside.

The server slipped by and nodded at the empty mugs. "I've got their bill covered." Jake gestured to Paul and Sandy's cups. Barry left that for you." He pointed to the money under the mug and held up his cup. "Another chai latte would be great."

The server winked, "All your witnesses are gone. We just got a tray of the vegan cinnamon rolls out of the oven…"

Jake stretched out his long legs under the table and scratched at his jaw. "You're the devil…" He grinned. "…and I like that. Sure!"

****

Jake stood and realized he was the only person left from the lunch rush except for the eccentrically dressed girl with her nose in a paperback. Her broad-brimmed straw hat hid her features. As he pushed his chair back under the table, the decorated straw hat came off to reveal a riot of red hair tied with pink bindings and beads. The young woman sat straight up and hooked her arms on the back of the low chair. "Do you know how hard you are to find?"

"What?" Jake looked around for the person to whom she was speaking.

"You… It's not like the universe has a mobile phone directory." She huffed and pulled her herself up to her full five feet.

"Do I know you?"

She slung her hobo bag over her shoulder and took an impatient step toward him. "I should hope to say. We shared breakfast … Tonopah?"

Jake bent down to her petite form. "Red?"

"At the table, you couldn't see my impressive physical stature." She gestured grandly then posed demurely. She tapped her forehead. "When you meet a girl, you make quite an impression."

Jake sat dumbfounded. "What?"

"Has someone boxed your ears today?"

"What do you want, Red? Why did you track me down?" Jake pulled out a chair, and she sat and pulled the plate with the huge glistening cinnamon roll to her.

Jake glanced at the server when he heard a pitcher of water drop and shatter. The server's expression was telling. She had just watched a chair move into the table on its own and a plate slide in front of the invisible occupant.

He turned his attention to Red. "Are you going to eat that or just hold it hostage while we talk?"

Red folded her hands primly on the table. She dressed in a decorated denim skirt with a Mexican style peasant blouse. Her earrings were temple bells, and her petite hands wore silver rings on every finger. Jake heard the delicate tinkling when Red's body moved in gestures.

The server watched wide-eyed as she mopped up the ice and water. Red bent over the roll and inhaled the sweet scent, then pushed the plate back to Jake with two fingers. "I'm on a mission. Eat up."

Jake accepted the plate and began unrolling the warm pastry. "You have my undivided attention. What is it?"

"Your Cricket is about to be poisoned. Her husband is communing with the dark arts. He's been feeding her a compound mixed by a rogue healer. I happen to know," she gestured with a swirl of her hand over her head, "Dr. Aloysius Baptiste has a demonic mentor. For the right price, Aloysius will mix anything. Right now, he's making her husband an elixir called Humana Malignas Dormancy. Used habitually it drives the spirit into a black hole. Used in increased amounts, it separates the soul from the body."

"You mean it's deadly?" Jake's hand with the cinnamon roll halted at his lips."

The server rushed to his side. "Do you have a cinnamon allergy? Did I hear you ask if this is deadly?"

Jake's jaw dropped, and he shook his head. "You know what they say about talking to yourself. I'm fighting with myself over sugar."

The server stepped back, "We use monk fruit for that recipe. It's all good." The server looked at the chair opposite him as it teetered on its uneven legs. Slowly, she stepped back to her station.

Jake returned his attention to Red and raised a scrutinizing brow. "Humana Malignas Dormancy? Deadly to humans?" He reiterated.

Red blew out a huff. "What else could malignant dormancy mean?"

Jake's heart squeezed inside his chest. "And he's feeding it to her now?"

Red drew lace gloves out of her purse. "He's been using it for at least thirty days. The energies say, he'll return from his next trip to St. Martin with a deadly dose."

Jake wiped the pastry's taffy off his lips. "So he gets the stuff in St. Martin. How can he get it into the country?"

Red pulled on the gloves, which were absent fingertips, swirled a finger through the sugary remnant on his plate and sucked the tip. "The murderer visits every month on the new moon. You know the new moon energy guides people to grow spiritually and manifest their desires. The dark arts use that same energy to help Cricket's husband manifest his visions for a future without her."

Jake pulled his mobile phone out and consulted the moon calendar. "Tuesday is the next new moon." Jake stared hard at Red. "I appreciate you going through so much to bring me this information."

Red leaned back in her chair and smiled. "It's an old wives' tale that spirits can't travel. We travel at the speed of thought. I like you, Jake, and I like your Cricket, I might hang around a while, see how this all turns out." She raised both her hands in a comically haunting pose and snickered. "But, I am not your spirit to call. I'm not your pet."

"I owe you big time, Red. Have you ever considered just walking into the light? I hear it's the best feeling possible."

Red's chin dipped, and she shrugged. "I have some debts I need to repay before I see that light." Jake began to speak, and Red leaned in to put her small hand over his lips. "I know you're the curious type. Don't give me a second thought. I'll leave you my diary." She caught her hobo bag from the side of the chair and held it close. Then she was gone.

Jake furtively redialed Joan's number and heard the same droning tone of an out of work line. In frustration, he finished his cinnamon roll without tasting it. He swallowed the last of the tea and looked at his sticky hands. He'd stop in the bathroom on his way out.

Chapter 16

Jake locked the bathroom's door and turned around to be sure there was soap at the sink. Cricket's golden-brown hair hit him in the face, and Jake staggered back, unprepared for her psychic onslaught. He shook his head in confusion. His astral meetings with her had never intruded on his waking life, but she was certainly determined now.

"Cricket, darlin', what are you…"

Cricket launched herself at him, ardor in high drive. "It's been hours! Now that you've made a wanton woman of me, I can't go days without my name on your lips."

She backed him against the fainting couch in the small room, and he toppled onto it. "You're name's been on my lips. You just haven't heard it because I've been trying…" His frenetic explanation was cut short when she straddled his hips and pulled at his sweater. Her lips nibbled at the ripples of his abdomen. "Cricket! I'm not at home right now."

"Let'em watch."

"Thankfully, there's no one watching, but if our luck runs out, someone will be pounding on the door."

Cricket paused her eager fingers on his jean's brass buttons. The tip of one forefinger slid between her pouting lips. "Does that mean you don't wanna play? Cuz I really wanna play."

Jake's temperature spiked. "Oh, I wanna play." He assured. "I wanna play so badly I probably won't be able to walk when I leave this room, but darlin', we can't do this right now."

She sighed heavily, laid a hot kiss on his lips, and straightened above him. "Well, okay, but we're gonna make this happen later, right?"

He pulled her back down into a slow, warm, deep kiss, and then sat up, cradling her against his chest. "You bet. Later tonight I'll be there. Will you be wearing this…" He lifted a nearly transparent wrapper. "It can't be very warm, but it's warming me up!"

"You like it?" Cricket scooted off his lap and twirled around.

A knock sounded on the door. "Jake? You okay in there?" Asked the server.

"Yeah…uh…sorry, just checking my phone…"

Cricket purred. "I'll have a surprise for you when we meet again. I hope that will make you anxious to see me."

He drew her close against him and kissed her forehead. "I'm always anxious to see you. Now get out of here before they break down the door."

Jake let the water run a little longer than necessary while he willed his tented jeans back into place. He carefully dried his hands and thanked the gods he'd had the wisdom to lock the door.

****

On his way home he redialed Joan Carroll's number. This time it connected.

114

Jake rushed from the Lyft to the covered porch of the historic Broderick Row home. After he rang the original brass doorbell, Jake leaned back and admired the elegant 'painted lady' that survived the 1906 earthquake. Joan Carroll swung back the heavy door after viewing him through the thick leaded glass window.

"Jake?" She stepped back and extended her hand.

"Joan?" He stepped onto a runner laid over gleaming original wood floors. "She's a beauty." He gestured around the ornate cornices and carved plaster reliefs in the archways. "She's fostered so much happiness. This house has been in the family for generations, right?"

Joan led him up the stairway, "It has, and I'm fortunate to be a family friend who lives in the mother-in-law suite upstairs."

"You are far too young to be a mother-in-law!" Jake appreciated the living areas they passed as the staircase switched from painted white and wood to ancient white paint approaching her top floor suite.

"You appreciate this stuff, don't you? How about a cup of tea?" Joan went to her stove and turned on the kettle to prepare a teapot. She gathered cups and led Jake to a small café table by a picturesque window.

"Rainy days call for tea. I enjoy architecture that has been preserved so you can feel the life in the home." Jake caught himself before he got too esoteric.

"I know Barry referred you to me. Have you had a recent loss?" Joan's tone was compassionate.

"Actually, Barry said you had information about a certain individual I might find helpful."

"I..." Joan turned from Jake and busied herself in a cupboard.

"I'm not asking for secrets. I know you're bound by regulations, but a woman's soul is in jeopardy. You hold the key to her survival." Jake watched Joan's posture turn inward, further away from him. "Barry said you'd have to decide if you could talk to me, but he thought you would."

Joan's hand covered her mouth as she placed everything but the teapot before him. "Have a seat. Who… are you talking about?"

Jake sat, reading her tense aura. "Asher Parks and his wife Constance."

Joan held on to the back of her chair and breathed out in relief. "Oh! I thought it was going to be someone I liked."

Jake's brows knit. "Seriously?"

Joan sat as her posture relaxed. "How have you been dragged into this?"

"I'm trying to protect his wife. We have a valid reason to believe he's poisoning her."

Joan's eyes closed and slowly reopened. "Barry believes this? Who is we?"

"Well," Jake shifted in his seat. "I have a couple of friends assisting me, and Barry of course, but when you get right down to it, I guess it's just me…"

"Why would you think Parks is trying to poison his wife?"

Jake bit at his lower lip. "A large percentage of your clients experience some sort of visitation from lost loved ones, isn't that right?" Joan nodded. "Do you believe those visitations are real or hallucinatory?"

After drawing in a deep breath, Joan looked up at him. "You're asking my personal opinion?"

"Yes."

"I believe they're real. The stories people tell are too consistent over every age, every religion, every continent throughout time. I think deniers are mired in fear of being ridiculed."

Jake looked up at her through his lashes. "I agree. Let's see if I can expand your beliefs further. Do you believe in astral travel? Communication between multiple planes of existence?"

Joan jumped as the kettle whistled. Her expression was cautious as she warmed the teapot, poured out that water and proceeded with the ritual of brewing tea in a pot. Jake's heel began to bounce on the wooden floor, and she cut him a sideways glance. "I've studied transpersonal psychology. I'm aware of different planes of consciousness, and I'm aware there are legitimate communicators with those considered to be dead." She made air quotes.

Jake kept his voice even and calm. "Then, I won't freak you out if I tell you, Constance Nielson, Parks' wife has been contacting me on the astral plane for the past six weeks." There was a beat of silence between them. "I believe he is deliberately keeping her comatose and now he's about to use a deadly compound of some kind that will look as though she's drifted to natural death."

Joan brought the teapot to the table, sat heavily in her café chair, and gave him a direct look. "Let me plainly share with you; I think you may be right. Of course, I didn't know about his use of this…compound." Joan poured tea into both cups.

Jake fell back in his chair as if the breath had been knocked out of him. "Give me a minute…"

Joan rested her hand on his forearm, "I meditate out there," she nodded toward her balcony. "Perhaps you'd like to be alone?" She led him to a small balcony with plants and a religious figure perched over a fountain. He followed her, and she left him there, closing the French door behind her.

****

Jake used a breathing exercise to regain a state of peace. He prayed for clarity and wisdom; his thoughts centered on Asher Parks. The world soft-focused in that space and glowed with a blessed light. Jake felt the air moving and heard the sound of fabric rustling. He opened his eyes to see an exquisite androgynous figure in a glowing robe. The breeze fluttered the angel's ebony dreadlocks around its shoulders. A calm smile spread across its golden face. "You have shown much love in this world. You seek to protect life."

"What about those I couldn't protect? Can you tell me about Asher Parks?"

"We have received the souls of those he sinned against."

"He killed them; how many?"

The angel's dark eyes glistened with tears. "He has dishonored the sixth commandment on five occasions."

The angel spread its arms wide, and the deaths played across its robe's ivory expanse. Jake covered his mouth. "How did Parks get away with murdering a college student, his parents, and Cricket's parents? He's heading for a sixth victim!"

The angel closed the panorama and folded its hands into its sleeves. "The Creator will see to him. The good news is, your love is the heart cord that will assist Cricket's awakening."

"We need the help of Cricket's cousin. Is he someone we can depend upon who will be true to her?"

"You will find his intentions are pure."

"Does that mean our efforts are blessed?"

"Good is always blessed, Jake." The angel's hands graced Jake's shoulders. "The Creator, who is Love, forever blesses, guides and protects you. The Creator's answer is always *yes*."

****

Jake opened the French doors as if he'd not just been speaking with an angel. Joan looked up from the book she had opened. "Did you get the answer you were hoping for?"

Jake smiled. "I believe so. I can't prove it yet, but, Parks has murdered before. He strangled a girl in college, murdered his parents by electrocution and Cricket's parents with a natural gas explosion."

Joan balked, "How can you possibly know that?"

"Spirit showed me each murder." Jake gestured to the balcony. "Now he's trying to murder Constance." Jake's complexion paled as he grasped his abdomen and sat to put his head between his knees. Joan ran for a damp dishtowel. Kneeling beside him, she placed it on the back of his neck and could feel the heat his pain generated.

"I'd suspected this, Jake, but I didn't know."

Jake pulled himself together and sat back on the sofa. "We'll need your help. Do you know the name of Constance's cousin who's trying to save the family business?"

She frowned with concentration. "I know his first name is Sam, and I know he was made the head of research and development after Constance's father died, though I believe he's functioning more like a CEO now. I know the name of the company is Nielson Artificial Intelligence."

"Okay, now I have the biggest ask of all. Barry needs to see this cousin. He'll undoubtedly give a police detective some credence, but you're the therapist who's been counseling the suspect. You have inside information. If you add your weight to

Barry's suspicions, the cousin may be much more willing to take on the role of power of attorney for Constance."

Joan took a few seconds to mull this over. "It would be better, ethically, if Barry and I approached her cousin together. If things go wrong, Parks could sue me over this."

Jake nodded slowly. "I guess this is one of those times we have to blindly trust spirit. Once we have custody of Constance and can prove she was poisoned, your worries go away."

****

Jake King was a man of faith; Joan had no question about that. She'd seen him interact with whatever he saw in meditation. She shivered. Whoever and whatever appeared to him dropped him to his knees. In the grey weather, Jake's face glowed with an otherworldly aura. He'd gone into the meditation on a fishing expedition and returned to her living room with absolute certainty. There was no doubt in her mind that Jake totally believed. *What do I do now?* She rang Barry.

****

The bar was brightly lit on a dreary day, and Joan caught Barry's eye as he entered. She waved the server over for another Irish coffee.

Barry stood, looking at her empty mug. "You started without me."

"You would have too if you saw what I saw."

Barry dropped into the opposite seat and motioned to the server for his Irish coffee. "Is it about your favorite psychopath?"

"No, it's more about your friend, Jake. His connection to spirit is impressive."

Barry cocked his head, "Huh?"

"I watched Jake go into a meditation." She gestured to the outside, "It was on my balcony, in misting rain, gray as it is right now. What happened next, blew my mind."

The server sat down the drinks. "So… what happened?"

"He closed his eyes, began his meditation, and held an actual dialogue with an entity. There was an exchange of light, and I couldn't look away from them." She looked down and stirred the whipped cream into her drink. "When he came back inside, he was a different man."

"In what way?"

"He'd gone out there disturbed and confused, but the confidence and knowledge he gained after that meditation changed his posture and expression. He *knew*. It was palpable."

Barry frowned and brought the cup to his lips. Joan smiled at the whipped cream on his brushy mustache. He licked it off and shrugged. "I've seen a lot of delusional people with absolute conviction in what they believe."

Joan held his gaze for a long moment. "Barry, delusional people, psychotics, they have disorganized thinking. Do you believe Jake has this type of thought?"

"No," he admitted slowly.

"Is his thought process in any way tangential or does he speak in word salad?"

"No." He admitted again.

"I know crazy when I see it. This young man is not crazy." She sipped her drink.

"Could he be running a con?" Barry's knuckles rapped the table.

"To what end?"

Barry rubbed his neck as if he head hurt. "Money? Fifteen minutes of fame?"

"What, the fame of being a psychic who rescued a woman from murder? I mean, if that's it, I'd think that was justified fame. But I don't see him as a con-man."

Barry's reply was reluctant. "No, that's the problem. It's all too fantastic to be real. But, dammit, I believe him enough to ask you to go with me to her cousin for that power of attorney."

For a beat of silence, Joan held his gaze. "I'll go with you."

$$Chapter\ 17$$

Jake could not wait to get a moment alone in his room to meet with Cricket. His mind held new facts, careful plans, and his hopes for their future. Facts and dreams whirled like an out of control kaleidoscope. He was so practiced in astral projection now, all he had to do was get quiet and think of her, and he was there.

It was their favorite tropical island. He could see the mountain cave high above him. When he looked around, he saw Cricket skinny dipping in a pool fed by a tumbling waterfall. Multicolored parrots bathed alongside her and preened in the shady tide pool.

"I've been waiting for you." She grinned as she surfaced close to him. "The water's just the right temperature. Let me help you." He looked down, and his clothes vanished.

"Nice trick." He chuckled. "How can I repay your service?"

She perched on a smooth, flat rock. "What comes to mind?"

He swam below her in the pool and caught each ankle in his hands. "I have some ideas."

Her shrieks startled the birds into flight and were replaced by sighs and moans.

Jake harbored masculine pride at the perfection of his performance. Cricket rested against him, boneless and sated. "I trust my lady was pleased by today's interlude?"

"Mmm. Very pleased. You may get a promotion."

"Madam is too kind." He ruffled her hair and sat up, drawing her with him. "We have to get serious for a few minutes, Connie. Does that name sound familiar?"

She cocked her head. "Kinda."

"Your name is Constance Nielson Parks. I don't know when they started calling you Cricket. Any of this ring a bell?"

Cricket frowned heavily, trying to remember, but shook her head no.

"I know where your husband is hiding you. You're married to a man named Asher Parks."

Cricket gasped. "Asher? Did I marry Asher? I couldn't have married Asher."

Jake sighed. "I don't know why you married him, because if you think he's a jerk, you're right. Even worse, he's a dangerous jerk. I'm coming to get you."

"You are? When?"

"We'll be coming for you in a day, two at the outside."

Her eyes grew large. "How?"

"Don't worry about that."

"But I do. I can't move. I can't help you."

"You don't have to worry about helping us. Except for this. You're beginning to be able to track with your eyes, right?"

"Yes."

"I want you to play possum for the next day until we get to you. Don't open your eyes, don't wiggle your toes, don't respond at all until you hear my voice."

"I can do that."

"Soon, darlin', very soon we'll be together, and all of this will be real for us."

Cricket blinked them out of their waterfall paradise, and within seconds had drawn him to her bedside on Gable Island. For the first time she stood in the middle of her sick room, wearing a simple hospital gown, her beautiful hair shorn, looking as wan and frail as she felt. Her gaze was cast down at the floor. "I want you to know, before you go further, what you're dealing with. Jake…" Her eyes were enormous in her ravaged face. "…are you sure you wouldn't be better off alone?"

Jake scooped her into his arms, and she whimpered against his gentle strength. "I love you, Cricket. You didn't get like this overnight. You probably won't come out of it overnight either. But with some help, you'll get better. You'll be your beautiful self once you're with people who love you."

Her eyes reflected the sadness of her world. "How long will that take? How long do you want to live with an invalid?"

He carried her to the cheval mirror. "This is what I see when I look at you." Her image transformed into the healthy, glowing woman she was with him. He turned her to face him. "This is the you I will always see. Now, and when we're both a hundred years old and leaning on our walkers. I'll also see you just this way while you're recuperating." Her look was skeptical. He kissed her forehead and went on. "You have to trust me, Cricket. You have to fight to live. Will you trust me?"

Cricket drew a shuddering breath. "Yes." She wrapped her arms around him and melted against his strength. "Yes. I love you too, sugar, and I will trust you."

Chapter 18

Nielson Artificial Intelligence turned its twentieth-century building on its ear by converting the atrium into a sea of undulating skateboard surfaces. Their Silicon Valley software developers blew off steam popping, grinding, and sliding on their breaks.

When Barry and Joan arrived at the reception desk, they were distracted by the view of what was essentially a skateboard park behind the receptionist. Barry Michaels flashed his detective's badge and announced they were there to meet with Sam Albright. "Or is he the guy out there on his board?" Barry nodded to an almost thirty-something guy on a worn skateboard.

"Mr. Albright is coming out of a board meeting on the fifth floor. I'll send you up."

Barry watched the elevator lights as they ascended. "I thought you said this guy was the head of R and D?"

Joan shrugged. "I suppose they made him CEO when Parks started trying to sell the company. Thank God there's a Board of Directors, or Parks would already have sold the company and Cricket would be dead."

The door swooshed open on an executive floor dated to the 1980s. A dignified assistant, a holdover from Mr. Nielson's era, greeted them before they even stepped off the elevator. "Mr. Albright is headed here now and asked me to get you settled in his office. May I offer you coffee, water, tea?"

They followed the attractive older woman. She escorted them to a traditional CEO's office. Award plaques intermingled with images of their prototypes in action. High concept photos of manufacturing and medical equipment decorated the walls.

"Nothing for me." Joan demurred.

Barry nodded, "I think I'm good; thank you."

Sam Albright was a good-looking though an understated man in his early thirties. He wore a blue blazer over his worn jeans as well as a scuffed pair of Adidas skate shoes. *Definitely a skateboarder.*

He strode into the room, already extending his hand to shake. "I was surprised when our head of security announced your visit. How can I help you? We have a situation involving the police?"

Barry introduced himself and Joan, flashing his badge again. "Mr. Albright, I suppose I have the perfect good news/bad news scenario."

Albright frowned as he removed his blazer to reveal a well-worn flannel shirt. "That needs an explanation."

"Yes, sir. We know you've been in a pitched battle with Asher Parks over the proposed sale of NAI. He wants the sale and the money, and with your cousin Constance out of the picture, he's got a reasonable chance of getting his way."

"That's right." Sam nodded as he sat behind the wide desk. "We've been fighting him in court for about six months now." Sam slid back and leaned his chair to cross one foot onto his knee. "He started looking for a buyer within a month of Cricket's accident." Sam made a shooting gesture with two fingers. "And that's not all. He's playing fast and loose with the figures on the sale." Sam hesitated for a beat. His left hand began a compulsive thumb and finger touching habit. "He's inflating his and Cricket's net worth and the worth of the company. Advising buyers that he's the CEO and empowered to make the sale. That's an assertion we successfully challenged in court." Sam brushed his hair off his forehead and shrugged. "We requested his tax returns since his marriage to Cricket, but so far he's stalled us on that. He has nothing in writing that gives him the power to make any decisions for NAI, but that's not stopping him."

Barry looked at Joan. At her nod, Barry spoke. "We think your cousin's life is at risk from Parks. If she's dead, he inherits everything, including legitimate rights to sell NAI. Because she's incapacitated, and you're her closest living relative, we're turning to you for help."

Albright sat heavily in his executive chair, unmoving. "Now, you'd really better explain."

After Joan concluded her recounting, Barry added a little more. "Since the story has been that Cricket's parents died in a gas explosion, I took the liberty of checking with Pacific Gas and Electric. They turned off the gas at the main for that house days before your aunt and uncle arrived, at your aunt's request. No one can prove she didn't turn it on again, herself. From what I understand about her habits, it seems unlikely. She always relied upon the experts to work with utilities."

Albright nodded, a grim expression playing about his lips. "Your inference is correct, Detective. Aunt Kathy was a smart lady. I know Parks always tried to portray her as a flighty socialite. That's not who she was. It scares me to think he took Cricket out of the hospital and has her on an island somewhere."

Joan leaned in. "Can you accompany us to court today? We need a protective order against Parks, and we need to move her to Stanford University Medical Center. To do that, we need you to assume power of attorney."

Albright cocked his head, "If it will save my cousin."

Barry nodded solemnly. "This is a do or die moment."

Albright stood, typing speedily on his cell phone. "Of course, let's head out now." He pocketed his car keys from the desk drawer and gave Joan a companionable look. "I want to thank you for being brave enough to bring this to my attention. The family never trusted Asher after we got to know him."

****

Asher Parks wasn't just warm, he was sweating furiously, and the heat wasn't only coming from the weather. The CIA was trying to access his brain again. *Don't they think I can feel it?* He despised the heat of St. Martin Island. There was a reason he lived in the cool, temperate climes of San Francisco. *That way, I can accurately tell when they're after my brain.* Trickles of sweat coursed down the back of his neck and dripped down his spine and into his pristine slacks.

The onboard entertainment monitor on the plane warned him through the headset that he was under close surveillance. The message seemed to be just for him since none of the other passengers looked alarmed, though they were all covertly scanning his appearance. He hated to sweat in front of others, hated to let them know the government was invading his thoughts. The one place he'd never been able to wear his protective clothes was on a plane. They wouldn't pass through the security check. He was reduced to virtual nakedness without his protective clothing until he could get to the men's room and change. All the people around him saw his victimization, and he knew it.

Outside the airport's main entrance, he glanced at the ragtag line of taxis. He didn't trust any of those people to get him to Dr. Baptiste's office. God knew if they were secretly working for the CIA. He picked up his backpack, and in the midday heat, headed down what passed for the coastal highway. Asher walked and dodged tour buses with travelers hanging over the sides, their cameras recording him. He was exhausted, unaccustomed to physical activity, sweating, and thirst.

Even his fears of the CIA didn't stop him from accepting a ride from an older island woman. She stopped her beater of a truck and offered him a lift -- for cash, of course.

The vehicle's suspension groaned every time it dodged a pothole and shrieked when it landed in one. The inside of the junky truck smelled of wet goat hair, and Asher hung halfway out the window, trying to avoid any contamination. She attempted to chat with him in broken, heavily accented English. He met each attempt with a wave of his hand and a shake of his head.

They were getting closer and closer to noisy bars and tourists ambling aimlessly with elaborate containers of liquor in their hands. After many such journeys, he recognized the aqua awning on the building a few blocks ahead that was Dr. Baptiste's clinic.

"Stop! Stop here." She slowed to a stop next to the paper-strewn sidewalk, and he peeled off a ten-dollar bill which brought a toothy smile laced with gold to her face.

"Merci, Monsieur."

Asher decided to take the broken concrete steps down to the beach and hoped the breeze off the ocean would blow most of the wet goat odor off him by the time he reached the clinic. He trudged along the golden sand, straw fedora falling into his eyes. The air hung like a damp beach towel.

Can they see me on the beach? He looked up to search the cloudless sky. *Am I a target? Satellites can identify a person from space. They read my thoughts on that damn plane. They know what I'm doing. If they could, they'd already have me in manacles...*

His foot caught on a large shell, and he hit the sand, face down, with a grunt. *Son of a bitch...* The sand smelled especially nasty here, and as Asher pushed himself up and turned his head toward the ocean, he knew why. Lying next to him, its eyes sunken and dead, was a decaying albatross.

An albatross. Holy God! A dead albatross. Could there be a worse omen in the world? He crabbed away from the dead bird. *It's the harbinger of doom. I'll have to move Connie, and I'll have to do it before they find her.*

He scrambled to his feet and brushing sand off his sports jacket; he dialed the Gable Island number. Nico answered the emergency cell phone. "They're coming for us, Nico!" Asher ranted. "Remember where I told you to put her?" Nico grunted a reply. "Do it now. I'm relying on you." Another grunt. Asher was never sure if he was getting through to this guy, but it was out of his hands now. He'd done all he could.

Chapter 19

Jake looked out at the light blue sky and snapped an image for his memory. The white clouds drifted across the smooth sea. The reflection was like cotton candy on glass. *Today is our first day together.* Their boat, followed by the Coast Guard cutter, and a marine ambulance, headed for Gable Island.

It was less than an hour's endeavor but seemed interminable to Jake. His heart raced as the Coast Guard skillfully threw the lines and secured the boats. The spiked adrenaline crawled up his spine as he restrained himself from bowling over the professionals to get to his woman. *Any minute. Any minute now, I'll have her.*

A man in a generic uniform took off for the far side of the island when the Coast Guard landed. Jake was the first man on the steps and up to the house, followed by Barry and the Coast Guard Officer, Commander Baum. Close on their heels were several paramedics carrying a stretcher and their gear.

Jake confronted the women who hung back at the open door. "Where is she?" He demanded.

The women made gestures of non-comprehension as they muttered, "No English."

Thundering footfalls followed as Barry, and the men searched the small house. Disappointed, Jake heard them calling to each other, "Clear!" and "No one here!"

Barry joined Jake in his interrogation of the women. He flashed his police badge. "Where is Mrs. Parks?" The woman who seemed to be the spokesperson looked at him with wide, fearful eyes. Barry turned to Jake. "What language do they speak?"

Jake snarled in frustration. "I don't know. I thought it was Spanish, and I was prepared for that, but they act like they don't understand."

Barry sized up the most likely talker and put on a tough, interrogator voice. "There's an empty hospital bed upstairs, medical containers and a bottle of pills with Mrs. Parks' name on them …Where is she?"

The women stared at him mutely. He turned to Commander Baum. "I want these people taken into custody for the kidnapping of Constance Parks. Radio ahead and tell them we need a translator. I'm not sure what…"

A young Coast Guard Seaman spoke up. "It's Portuguese, sir."

Barry turned on him with a pleased smile. "You speak it?"

"No sir, only a couple of words, but I know it's Portuguese."

"Good man! Tell them we need a Portuguese translator asap upon arrival."

Jake turned to the detective. "I still feel she's here."

Barry clapped a sympathetic hand on his shoulder. "We've searched every inch of the place, son; we couldn't find anything. She was obviously moved in one big hurry but where to?" Barry shrugged. "Hopefully one of these women will tell us…"

"Where was her room? Maybe I can pick up something there."

Barry pointed. "Top of the stairs, on the left. Hope your Spidey sense gives us a clue."

Jake climbed the squeaking stairs to Cricket's room. Dread encircled him. He didn't need a psychic sense to see that she'd been transported abruptly. Rumpled sheets lay on a hospital bed slightly askew, drawers and cabinets hastily left open were a dead giveaway. His worst imaginings worked overtime. He imagined Cricket, helpless and unresponsive in a heap in the bottom of a boat, at the top of the lighthouse, or on the craggy shores of the island waiting for an outgoing tide.

His heart hammered as he reached into the Universe for her. A very faint sense of her came back. It was as if he visualized her through a fog. He couldn't believe she was anywhere except on the island, unless -- his pulse escalated, she was on a boat.

Shaking with foreboding, Jake made his way downstairs. Barry and the Coast Guard commander spoke together at the bottom of the stairs. Jake interrupted with a hand to Barry's shoulder.

"They took her away in a big hurry and not too long ago. But I can't read where. It's almost like she's drugged and can't respond to me. We need to search every inch of the island." He turned to Commander Baum. "I think you need to launch a search for any boats nearby. She could be alone in an unmoored boat."

"You mean set adrift?"

"Yes." Jake sighed deeply. "It's a possibility. Did you have any luck talking with the nurses?"

Barry gritted his teeth. "I think at least one of them would love to tell us where she is, but see the big guy over there? They're terrified of him."

Jake stalked into the room where the nurses stood cowering, and one large and forbidding man, who was the muscle, watched everything with a defiant glare. "Please." Jake began. "I know you've cared for her for months. If you know where Mrs. Parks is, you must tell us so we can take her to a hospital."

A young, petite woman looking terrified but determined, began timidly. "Senhor…"

Jake turned to her and took her hands. "I swear to you, I'm here to help her. Please tell us where he's put her."

"Sim…" She whispered.

The young seaman nodded in her direction. "I know that much. She means yes."

The angry man in the back of the room issued a gruff, and rapid-fire rebuke and the young woman paled, turned away, and refused to say more. Barry and Commander Baum conferred for a moment. Commander Baum stepped forward. "We can't wait any longer, or we'll lose the light. You two men search the lighthouse and any other structures. You," he gestured to another group, "search every inch of this island. I'll radio for a helicopter to identify any boats in the area that appear to be adrift. You medics check the house again, and Seaman Suny, you guard these prisoners. No one leaves this room."

"Yes, sir."

It was encroaching on seven-thirty in the evening before every team returned with a disheartening report. Barry led Jake away from the crowd and let him know the search had to stop for tonight. "That doesn't mean interrogations will stop. I'll isolate the young one, who wanted to tell us something, and I'll have an interpreter to help me convince her to talk. Why don't you go home and get some rest?"

"You think I can rest?" He shook his head. "No. I'll stay here tonight. I know she's here somewhere, Barry. I'll keep looking."

****

No one among the Portuguese group would spill the details. In the threatening darkness on deck, when the cutter hit a wave, someone managed to knock their star witness unconscious. The other women of the group cast reproachful glances at the strong man in their midst. He sat stoically unperturbed.

"Medic, see to this woman!" The Commander ordered. "Separate each prisoner and give them a one-to-one guard. Put two-to-one on the big guy. I'll be damned if this jerk is going to stop one more witness from telling what she knows."

****

The danger of the water is isolation. Jake surveyed the island's distance from San Francisco as he recalled Desmond's freaky channeled revelations from weeks ago. *The danger of earth is the distance.* Jake shook his head. *Asher got me on that. The danger of air is its absence.* Jake prayed; *Please tell me she's not buried alive on this island.* Jake looked at the dry scrub on the craggy island and shivered at the thought of the last prediction. *The danger of fire is the destruction of evidence.*

Before midnight, he began his meditation, Cricket's location was pitch dark. He finally connected with her! He couldn't see her, but he could feel her frail body and wrap her in his protective embrace.

"Where are you, darlin'? Can you see anything?"

"I can't. And it's so cold in here, Jake. I was asleep, and I woke up. Where am I?"

"I think you're still on the island. We haven't been able to find you, but I'm still looking. Don't worry, darlin'. I will find you."

"I'm so tired." She mumbled. "I think they gave me something. I'm sorry, sugar, I can't stay awake…"

****

Barry looked up from the soda machine. He got one for himself and one for the woman he was about to interrogate with the help of an interpreter. His partner for the last five years stood by expectantly.

"Any success?"

Barry shook his head. "Just about to start. The big, burly guy in room seven managed to give our best witness a concussion on the way over from the island. Interviewing her is out for the night, she's at San Fran General. He won't talk, I'm sure, but have a go at him if you want."

His partner winked. "It so happens my Avo was Portuguese. I know a few threatening words in that language…" He opened the door to interrogation seven while Barry headed into his own room.

****

At first light, Barry and Commander Baum stood together on the deck of the cutter as they sped toward Gable Island. "Any information on the whereabouts of Mrs. Parks?" Baum asked as the two men ducked into the cabin.

"No one's talking. Isn't it ironic, Parks gave his muscle an emergency number? An attorney showed up for all of them, and they're not breaking their silence."

"Well, I've had an idea." Baum patted an instrument that looked something like a large digital camera. "This is a thermal imaging sensor. We point it at walls; it will show us if there's a body with a heat signature behind them. If there's a hiding place in one of the structures on that island, we'll find her."

The seas were a bit higher today, but they managed. Commander Baum and Barry left most of their men cooling their heels by the pier as they made their way up to the house with the EMTs and the heat sensor.

****

They found Jake in the upstairs hall tapping on walls and listening for any sound change that might indicate a hollow space. "I started in the basement, but the walls are cement, and it echoes so badly down there I can't hear anything." Jake led Barry, a little way from the group. "I contacted her last night and then again early this morning. She's more awake now, which isn't saying much. All she can say is that it's completely dark where she is, and she's cold, hungry and thirsty."

"Uh, sirs, I think we should get started," the head EMT encouraged. "It's been at least twenty-four hours since she was moved yesterday. Depending on when he moved her, Ms. Parks could be approaching dehydration. She could be in danger of having a seizure without her medication. Time is of the essence."

"I was just catching up with Mr. King about the searches he's conducted overnight." Barry turned to Jake. "Commander Baum has brought a little toy we think will help. Let's start up here."

****

Jake was a knot of impatience as Commander Baum moved methodically from one wall to the next. The images were jaw-dropping. They could see rats scurry from their nesting place and traverse along the pipes inside the walls. They did not, however, see a woman. The hour dragged into two and then three as they continued the fruitless search.

"Look! I've had enough." Jake cried in exasperation. "I told you, I sound-tested every wall except the basement. The basement is where we need to go."

Commander Baum shot him a doubtful look. "Protocol states…"

"I agree with Mr. King, sir." The head EMT spoke up. "Time is very much of the essence now. Let's try the basement."

Baum sighed. "Okay. Let's move down there."

Jake led the men down the wooden basement stairs and waited in an agony of worry as they reset the equipment. He looked at the moisture collecting on the cement walls and shivered slightly. Upstairs was cool; the basement was downright cold.

Commander Baum moved methodically around the walls of the subterranean room, and on the far wall, tucked behind the stairs, they finally saw something.

What could only be Cricket's small form showed a heat signature. There was a slight debate about whether they should hunt for a mechanism that opened the hidden door. Commander Baum cut through the handwringing, ordering his men in with a jackhammer and tire irons. Fifteen minutes later, in a cloud of dust with splintered wood and chunks of cement underfoot, Jake scrambled to Cricket's side. She lay on a rickety gurney, unresponsive but shivering, in a thin hospital gown.

Jake reached out to snatch her up, and one of the EMTs stopped him. "Let them search her first, sir. She could be on a booby-trap."

Jake froze in horror. *Surely not!* But he agreed. *Better safe than sorry.* The safety check took only minutes and once satisfied, she was safe to move, the EMTs rushed in with blankets and all their equipment. They did a cursory exam.

The paramedic pulled his stethoscope from his ears and looked around at Jake. "She seems pretty stable, though unresponsive and cold." He frowned. "Her BP's a little low. Probably from dehydration."

Jake let out his held breath. "May I touch her?"

"Sure." The paramedic made room for him while he and his crew prepared Cricket for transfer.

"Hey, Darlin', any time you wanna bat those beautiful eyes at me, I'm ready."

The paramedic gave him a dubious look. "Uh, if you'll step back, sir, we need to transfer her to the gurney now."

"Oh, yeah. May I ride with Cricket? I mean, at least till we get to the shore ambulance?"

"Yes, sir. Just give us a few minutes to get her situated, and you can sit beside her all the way back." They wrapped her in silver shock blankets, put chemical warming packs alongside her and wrapped her head in a thermal blanket.

Barry snapped pictures of everything in Cricket's sick room, and the hideaway in the basement. The paramedics and Coast Guard swept the cabinets and tables for every medication bottle they could find. Barry pointed at the tube feeding bags. "Take those too. I wanna know the contents of every one of those bottles and bags of formula. Send samples of everything; I mean everything we collect to the police lab and poison control. The rest can go with her to the hospital. We'll see if what the lab finds matches the labels on the medications."

Chapter 20

Cricket's hand felt smooth and well cared for when Jake was allowed to sit beside her on the ride back to San Francisco. "Hey, beautiful! We're almost home. Parks will never get to you again."

Jake stared at her placid, unlined face that in repose seemed much too thin. He struggled to believe this lifeless woman could be his Cricket. Jake reached out to her psychically and got empty static. He'd never experienced a time when he reached static. *What is going on?*

****

Cricket found herself in a rolling meadow. She saw Jake searching for her, only a few feet away, but when she tried to run to him, an invisible barrier repelled her. She bounced off the obstacle, and it boinged like flexing plexiglass. It only took a few attempts before she resigned herself to its power over her, a limiting power she'd never faced before in the astral. *What is going on?*

A soft nicker sounded behind her and Cricket turned to find Prince, her Connemara pony gently prodding her backside with his muzzle. Prince died when she was fourteen, leaving a hole in her heart; no other creature had ever filled. Her eyes grew wide. "Prince?"

The pony blinked knowing brown eyes with long lashes. "Cricket, I wouldn't try to break through like that."

She rubbed her shoulder. "What is that thing? Why can't I get to Jake?"

Prince nudged her along a suddenly appearing path. "Walk with me."

She turned and ran a palm down his beloved face. "What are you doing here?"

"I came to see you." She smiled and scratched the edge of his cheek, a gesture he loved, just as if ten years and the grave had never separated them. "You looked like you could use some direction on the trail."

She slanted a look at him. "How are you talking to me?"

Prince laughed. "Well, I always talked to you. You know that. On the other side, there are no language barriers, so it's easier to talk telepathically. I came to help you."

"I've missed you so much, Prince!" Tears filled her violet eyes. "I wish I could stay here with you."

"Don't worry; we'll be together again before you know it. For now, I think you have work to do, and I can help."

"I don't understand any of this." She glanced around. "This is my astral world, right? Why can't I control it?"

Prince nudged her good-naturedly. "It is an astral plane, but it doesn't belong to you – or anyone else. You can't control it because you're conflicted. You can't live in two places at once."

Cricket pursed her lips. "You don't talk like a pony." She accused suspiciously.

"Maybe, I'm a very wise pony."

"Maybe, but still…"

Prince tossed his head. "Well, you're half right. I'm partly pony and partly…more. I'm a nice combination, don't you think? Who better to hear hard truth from than a beloved entity from your childhood?"

Cricket considered. "But you are part Prince, right, I mean, this isn't some con game?"

Prince nickered. "Prince very kindly allowed me to blend with his energy to speak with you. He loves you very much."

"Okay, then, what is the hard truth you need to tell me?"

****

As much as Jake would have liked to continue trying to reach Cricket on any level, the necessities of her medical care took priority. Before he could protest, she was whisked through to the emergency room, and doctors and nurses were everywhere. They drew samples of blood and what seemed like every other possible body fluid. The gurney barely stood still before she was off to a series of scans and electroencephalograms, leaving Jake helpless in the hospital waiting room. Sandy sat by his side.

She touched his arm lightly. "I know this has to be frustrating because your lines of communication are down."

"I've always been able to reach her. She didn't respond at all when we moved her."

"This isn't a fairytale. Did you expect Cricket to open her eyes and wake up because Prince Charming kissed her lips?"

Blood drained from his face. "I guess so. I don't know what to do."

"Be patient, buddy. It's only been a couple of hours. Let's see what the doctors can tell us. In the meantime, I met Sam Albright, Cricket's cousin, as they were bringing her in. I want you to meet him."

****

In the chapel's subdued lighting, Jake waited in the front pew, head down, in reflection. The door opened, and he heard Sandy's whispered words. Looking back at the closing door, Jake saw a thirtysomething young man with Cricket's coloring walk toward him. Jake moved over, and the young man sat.

"Sam?"

****

The conference room at Stanford Medical was a step above the chrome and fake walnut of most hospital conference rooms. Here the polished walnut was real, but Jake couldn't shake the feeling he was inside some movie of the week. Cricket had a team of doctors, overseen by Dr. Clark. The non-medical people included himself, Barry, and Sam. Barry brought along a sympathetic assistant district attorney.

The pathologist took the lead in explaining their findings. "Ms. Parks' tissues and stomach contents contain a modest amount of a substance called tetrodotoxin. It's sometimes referred to as the zombie drug. It's found most often in pufferfish. I'm sure you've all heard stories about Japanese pufferfish, and how some diners die each year from eating them? Even modest amounts, over time, will prove deadly."

The A.D.A., identified as Hua Yang, stood in alarm, her delicate complexion alive with red blotches of anger. "How in the world did that toxin get into Ms. Parks' bloodstream?"

The doctor snapped on gloves and held up a clear plastic bag containing a thirty-milliliter bottle with a dropper cap. "This was in Ms. Parks' medications. It's from a foreign provider, we think from somewhere in the Caribbean, it's marked vitamins. There are some vitamins in it. Unfortunately, it's predominantly tetrodotoxin. They were putting it in her tube feedings."

"Seriously?" She scribbled a note to herself. "What, are we dealing with a James Bond villain?"

Barry looked up and frowned. "Maybe an insidious serial killer."

Jake slapped his hand on the table for attention. "As much as I want to see justice done, I'm more interested in getting Cricket well. Where does she stand medically?"

Dr. Prasad, the hematologist, stood. "First, we need to flush the toxin from her system. There's not a huge amount of study on victims of tetrodotoxin poisoning. Not that many survive it. If victims receive enough medical support, they recover without further impairment. I suggest we attempt to purify her blood with plasmapheresis and her tissues with chelation therapy."

Cricket's cousin Sam nodded. "Whatever you need to do, whatever you think is best, I'll sign the papers."

Jake blinked back tears. "What about her mind?"

The neurologist handed out papers. "Ms. Parks' record shows that approximately four months ago, she suffered a skull fracture and brain swelling immediately after her auto accident. As might be expected, she was in a comatose state for approximately twenty days. When she returned to consciousness, her doctors kept her in a medically induced coma for another few weeks to help her heal. During that medically induced coma, her husband announced he was taking her to Switzerland for further treatment. He was advised not to take her anywhere by plane and certainly not to Switzerland because of altitude effects on brain injuries. He checked her out of the hospital against medical advice."

Sam raised his hand, "Asher made a big deal about Switzerland. He told the family he had a scientist building a special transport that would keep her stable at high altitude. We thought it was hokum."

Barry shook his head, "And all he did was take her to a secluded island."

The neurologist nodded. "She was looked after by a team of Brazilian nurses. All the prescription bottles are labeled by a French physician on St. Martin. We believe he is the man who compounded the vitamins containing tetrodotoxin.

A.D.A. Yang wrote in her notes. "During the four months she was on the island, her brain slowly healed on its own?"

Dr. Prasad nodded, "It appears the only thing keeping her unconscious is the tetro."

Yang clicked off her pen, and her brows rose indignantly. "We can extradite from St. Martin, in fact, we must. If Dr. Baptiste is giving this to Parks, who knows what else the doctor is doing?"

'It drives the spirit into a black hole.' Jake remembered Red's words when she told him of the poisoning. *Humana Malignas Dormancy.*

The neurologist spoke up, "Our EEGs show she is predominately in a Theta state which indicates deep relaxation and sleep. She also frequently dreams. Until the tetrodotoxin has been eliminated from her system, we suggest tried and true, non-invasive measures. I suggest music, family participation in reading and talking to her, physical therapy to keep muscles active, and so on."

Jake persisted. "So, in a lot of ways, you're saying her body has already healed itself?"

The doctors nodded in agreement. Dr. Clark stood. "Mr. King, my specialty is rehabilitative medicine. We're not going to know exactly how much neurological damage was done by the head injury until she's awake. Any time a patient is bedbound in the way Ms. Parks is, there are significant problems to be overcome. The good news is, her nursing staff were quite competent. Their daily exercises helped keep her muscles from contractures. They seem to have prevented pneumonia and bedsores. If she has the will and cognitive ability to work at it, I believe we can have her physically active again in a month."

Jake turned to the representatives of the legal system. "What can we do to take Parks out of the picture?"

Yang sat fuming, "Let me make some phone calls. Detective Michaels, will you please notify Homeland? We need to catch Parks bringing this into the country."

Barry took out his phone, "I'm on it."

Yang turned to Jake, "This is a complicated case, Mr. King. We don't want to swing and miss, let's not show him our playbook before we're ready to take the mound. We need to precisely follow police procedure, gather evidence, and take it to a Grand Jury. We don't want him to get away, but I fear that will leave him in the community longer than you would like. You do have a protective order against him?"

"For all the good that will do," Barry muttered. "Luckily she's got enough money for an army of guards."

****

Cricket rode Prince bareback, laughing as he galloped across the meadow. He dropped into a walk, and she sighed. "I couldn't stand my life if I couldn't come to the astral for an escape."

149

Prince bobbed his head in agreement. "It's necessary to the mortal psyche to have this release. You realize you could stay with us on this side. Only your desires compel you to go back to the physical. There's no judgment in staying here. However, if you choose to go back to your Jake, you must also choose to limit your time in the astral."

Cricket grew solemn. "You don't understand how awful the mortal experience is for me right now. It's the worst bondage you can imagine."

Prince's mental voice was compassionate. "We do understand. We also tell you, the striving to break free from your prison is what will propel you back to consciousness. It will not be easy, dear one."

Prince meandered them into a pool of shimmering water. Cricket slipped from his back and let the stimulating waters flow over and around her. She surfaced. "My biggest fear is that I'll be unable to recover."

Prince's voice echoed around her. "You will recover if it is your desire."

She stepped from the pond, suddenly knowing she bathed in healing waters. Feeling invigorated and fortified, she looked into Prince's compassionate chocolate eyes. "I'm ready. What must I do first?"

"Thinking plus feeling equals a healing." Prince advised. "Spend your time in your physical body. See yourself as awake. Strive to respond to your caregivers. Feel yourself alert and alive and interacting with your love. You may visit us here for a brief period nightly, but you may no longer stay unless you choose to cut life's silver cord."

Chapter 21

Miami, Florida

Asher Parks barely contained his rage at being detained at the Miami Customs Office. "As an American citizen, I have the right to life, liberty, and the pursuit of happiness. Happiness starts with my health, and you are threatening to take away my vitamins. They were specially formulated for me by my physician."

The Customs Officer was impassive. "You have two options, Mr. Parks, you can destroy the unidentified product, or you can stand here and argue with me and be fined…"

"I can afford to be fined. I can't afford to be without my vitamins."

"At any point did I say you'd be fined, and you'd keep those vitamins? No, you can dispose of them yourself, by placing them in the provided container, no harm no foul. Or, you can insist on coming into the United States with them, at which point we'll fine you *and* confiscate them. The attempt to bring in non-FDA approved medications will go on your permanent record. It's up to you."

Asher ground his teeth, knowing he couldn't dispose of the tetrodotoxin laced vitamins without gloves, and how would he explain that? "I've been through Customs with these multiple times and never had a problem. Why now?"

"The FDA is coming down on citizens seeking unapproved medical treatment. New regulations. You're holding up the line. What'll it be?"

Asher knew he was out of options. "Fine. Where shall I put them?"

The Customs Agent opened the neck of a red bag marked Hazardous Medical Waste. "In here, please, sir." Asher complied begrudgingly. "Now, if you'll follow me, please, we need to search the rest of your luggage."

Asher followed, sputtering his protests, while the Agent handed him off to another, even grimmer looking authority.

The Agent stopped at a wall phone. "He's dropped his load." He reported to his supervisors. "Yeah, it's secure, no one touched it. I'm sealing it and marking with my initials now for a chain of evidence. You have Feds ready to receive?"

****

"You can't do this to me! I'm an American citizen." Asher roared when the customs agent tore into his thousand-dollar sports coats with a seam ripper.

The Senior Supervisory Customs Agent spared a flinty glance at the entitled jerk making the threats against him. "I'm well aware of your nationality, Mr. Parks." He snapped. "I'm also aware you were trying to enter the country with contraband and verbally abused my agents when they stopped you. If I were you, I'd fall back on your right to remain silent."

"I want my attorney!" Asher demanded. "You'll all be very sorry you messed with me!"

"Uh-huh. My agents have called the number you gave us. This is the weekend. Maybe your attorney isn't as eager to hear from you as you imagine. Meanwhile, may we offer you a soft drink from the machine and a seat in the interrogation room?"

Asher fumed while crossing his arms over his chest. "I have nothing more to say."

"Good. Then you can wait there quietly. Grape soda?"

****

An agent from Homeland Security knocked on the window of the holding room door. "Excuse me, please," the Supervisor said. "Officer Ramirez, this man is not to go anywhere unobserved. Not even to the bathroom."

The Supervisor met his counterpart in the hallway. "What did you find, Ed?"

The tall man with the perpetually haggard face nodded. "Tetrodotoxin, just as predicted. This is a lethal dose, Butch. We have a hazmat team scrubbing down our lab as we speak. I don't know what that son of a bitch is up to, but it's gonna earn him a stay in Miami-Dade Pretrial Detention."

The Supervisor quirked a brow. "I don't think he's going to be very happy about that. And by the way, you should see the stuff he has sewn into his clothes! The jackets are lined with Kevlar fabric, and the hats, wait for it…the hats are lined with thin sheets of lead. We liked to never cut through the stuff. He have an assassin problem?"

Ed laughed. "Or maybe he's just nuts? Whatever, we don't know what he was planning to do with the drug, so we'll keep him in solitary for now. I suppose he's got a high-powered mouthpiece?"

"Yeah. But whoever that is doesn't seem too eager to get involved. Not that I blame them. What an asshole."

****

Jake's gaze darted back and forth over the gauges of the plasmapheresis machine. He watched the blood making its way into and out of the IV looking thing in Cricket's neck. Her nurse closed a series of clamps on the blue line, and then the red line, and flushed both with syringes. She pushed the machine back from the bedside and turned to Jake. "Well, sir, that's the last of the five treatments. I sure hope it works for her."

"Thanks." Jake acknowledged and watched her wrestle the machine out of the room.

Tomorrow they'll begin chelation therapy. I've got a few hours until they start her afternoon physical therapy. Jake tried to boost his spirits by hanging on to anything positive the doctors and staff told him. *The reports from the neurologist have been promising.* Cricket opened her incredible violet eyes, but she didn't track or give him any indication she knew he was there. The neurology team said they saw an improvement in her EEGs. Jake tried to temper his growing frustration with optimism.

He looked down on the faded beauty in the bed and waved a slice of star fruit under her nose. He swabbed fruit and sangria across her lips. *Maybe she'll recall our time in the island cave. Nothing. No reaction.* He blotted her lips.

Next, he reached for the vanilla and cream body lotion Sandy swore would entice the dead. He slathered the sweet-smelling stuff liberally on her delicate skin. She remained unresponsive.

Collapsing into the chair at her bedside, Jake held her hand urgently in his own. "What, Cricket? What must I do to see your soul behind those beautiful vacant eyes?" Tears came to his own eyes, and he ruthlessly blinked them away. "I've done everything I can think of. I can't reach you here. I can't reach you on the astral. Where are you?" No response. He stood and urgently shook the bedrails. "Cricket, damn it! Wake up!"

Jake felt hands on his shoulders. "C'mon Jake; you need a break." It was Sandy, drawing him away. "C'mon. We have a lunch date. Cricket is fine. Let's go."

Jake got up and followed, his emotions lingering at Cricket's bedside.

****

Thinking plus feeling equals a healing. Cricket reminded herself again and again. God knew she thought about Jake endlessly and felt the desperate need to drag herself into wakefulness.

Not desperation, dear one. Cricket heard Prince's mental voice. *Desire. Determination. Desperation draws you away from your goal. Belief in a thing makes it happen. That's right.* She knew that.

Just let it happen. She admonished herself.

****

Jake slumped into the fifth-floor waiting room chair, listening to Sandy's well-intentioned lecture. "I don't know the answers to the whys. I don't know why you could once reach her psychically and now you can't. I don't know why the doctor's say her EEG is improving when she's not waking up. But it's been days now, and we don't see any change. I think you have to prepare yourself for the possibility that she's lost out there in the cosmos and she's never coming back…"

Jake stood, fury coursing through him. "The Creator always says yes, Sandy! That's what I was told. The Creator always says yes, and I'm going to believe that."

"Jake, yes, can take a lot of forms. What if her yes isn't your yes? What if her healing is on the other side?"

Jake held his breath for a moment as if he'd received a blow, and then let it out. "If her healing is on the other side, I'd be okay with that. Oh, I mean, I'd hate it, and I'd miss her, but she'd be where she was supposed to be. She wouldn't be half in and half out of the world."

Sandy shook her head. "Is that for you to say? If you do everything, there is to do, and nothing changes…"

Jake squared on her; his fingers splayed on his hips; his stance authoritative. "We haven't even begun to do everything yet. We're just getting started. Look, I know this is hard to watch. You go ahead and walk away if you want. I'm not giving up; I'm not leaving her, I'm not…"

"Jake!" Cricket's day nurse ran into the waiting room just as Sandy opened her mouth to respond. "Jake! Come quick! Cricket opened her eyes, and she's tracking!"

Chapter 22

Palo Alto, California

Jake slid to a stop at Cricket's bedside. "Were you calling me?" She croaked through a dry throat.

"Yeah, darlin', I was. You've been asleep way too long." He looked up at the nurse. "Can she have some water?"

"How about ice chips? We'll try that first. I'll be right back with that, and I have to call the doctor."

"Thanks."

Jake turned his complete attention to Cricket. She felt as if he was visually eating her up. "Where am I? Are you real?" She whispered.

"Yeah, darlin', I'm real. You are awake. You're in Stanford Medical Center, and you're getting better every day."

"That's good." She found it hard to focus on anything but his face. "I feel strange. Does this bed raise higher? Can I sit up?"

Jake hedged. "Let's ask the nurse when she comes back."

The nurse returned, followed by two others and a Fellow in Neurology who turned to Jake. "Excuse me, Mr. King, we're going to interrupt you two for a few minutes to examine Ms. Parks."

Jake nodded. "Do what you need to do. I'm staying right here."

The doctor grinned. "We won't be long."

Cricket took her eyes off Jake's for a moment and looked at the nurse. "I'm so thirsty…"

"Let's try this." The nurse popped a minuscule piece of ice in her mouth.

"Oh, that's heaven." Cricket closed her eyes appreciating the cold wetness.

The nurse looked up at the doctor. "She's handling it okay. A little more ice?"

The doctor nodded, listening carefully to Cricket's chest.

The nurse turned to Jake and handed him the cup and spoon. "Tiny little pieces, very slowly." She admonished.

The exam seemed to Cricket to take forever, though, in reality, they were done in a matter of minutes. The nurses left the room, and the doctor asked her to follow his finger with her eyes, which was harder than she thought. "I'm so tired." She murmured, fighting to keep her eyes open to look at Jake.

"It's okay to rest," Jake assured her. "I'm not going anywhere. I'll be right here when you wake up."

Her eyes slid closed, and she slept the first natural sleep she'd had in months.

****

Her nurse promised to stay at Cricket's bedside while Jake went to talk to the legal team. "I don't want her to wake up and think I'm gone. You'll tell her, right?"

"You go on, Jake. Don't worry. I'll take care of Cricket." The nurse assured him.

Barry Michaels, dressed in blue jeans and a Grateful Dead tee shirt, discussed some papers with A.D.A. Hua Yang. Sam walked in, followed by a young man in a business suit who Jake immediately knew was a soldier.

"Casual day?" Jake asked, nodding at Barry.

"First day of retirement." Barry corrected. "Though I did put on a suit and tie this morning for a photo op." He slid a thin leather I.D. wallet at Jake who picked it up.

"Barry Michaels, Private Investigator." Jake gave an impressed nod. "Very classy."

"You'll understand the need for it in a minute," Barry grumbled before Sam interrupted.

"Everyone, this is LaVon Jefferson." Sam gestured to the tall, impressive black man with the military bearing. "He's agreed to head up the protective team guarding Cricket."

Jake extended his hand. "Your help is much appreciated, Mr. Jefferson. We have a rather bizarre set of circumstances here."

"Yes, sir, Mr. Albright briefed me. You and your lady will be safe with my men and me."

"Please, I'm Jake. We'll be working closely together."

"Okay. I'm Von. Happy to work with you. I heard Ms. Parks had a breakthrough today…"

"What?" Yang blurted. "Cricket's awake?"

"Yes, she is." Jake beamed. "Awake. Alert and she knows us."

Barry nodded. "That's great news, son, the best! I only wish we had the same."

Jake took a hesitant step back. "They're not taking away protective custody, are they?"

"No, no. They can't do that." Barry assured him. "But they're not doing much more." Barry gestured at the chairs.

"Everybody have a seat. Hua and I have a story for you. We went to a meeting with the San Francisco D.A. and the Chief of Police this morning. To make a long story short…"

****

"And that's it?" Jake fumed, "They can do that? It's not politically expedient, and hard to prove in court, so we're not even going to try?"

"We're not asking for a grand jury until we have solid evidence against Parks." Hua sighed. "That doesn't mean we'll stop pursuing the evidence. Without the city behind us, it will make it harder and longer."

"Right." Barry nodded. "I got my P.I. License so I can investigate what happened to the Parks and Nielsons and Cricket."

"You'll have all the financial support you need," Sam assured them. "And Mr. Jefferson, that goes for you too."

"Oh, one last thing I thought you might get a kick out of…" Hua ducked her head with a shy smile. "My law school roommate wound up working for the IRS. I gave her a call today and told her to look into the financial affairs of Asher Parks."

Sam grinned hugely. "Asher made false statements to insurers and banks. That's not just tricky business practice, that's illegal."

Hua nodded enthusiastically, "My friend at the IRS intends to freeze his accounts as soon as tomorrow. That young man may think he's going to flee the country before we can catch him. I hope he has diamonds buried on that island."

Jake roared with laughter. "Because he's frozen out everywhere else?"

"Exactly."

Chapter 23

Marin County, California

Asher was met at the San Rafael private airport by Tabitha Daniels, his 'special friend' and San Francisco Assistant District Attorney. The airstairs led him into her waiting arms. He gave her a sound kiss and turned to Senator Broadman who came down the stairs behind him. "This is the young woman who is responsible for contacting you and getting me out of that hell hole."

Senator Broadman extended his hand. "You must be Tabby."

"Hello, Senator." Her voice was low and throaty. "Thank you for coming to Asher's aid so quickly. I knew they had no grounds on which to hold him, but your involvement hastened his release by days, I'm sure."

"My pleasure to assist. Call on me any time you need my help." He turned to Asher. "My campaign manager will be in touch with you about that donation, Parks. Your support is much appreciated."

Asher and Tabby watched the squat, round man amble toward his limo. "What a toad," Asher grumbled. "I know you were the power behind my release. Thank you, Tabby. I don't know what this country has come to."

"Of course. It was a frivolous case, to begin with. They had no way of proving you knew what was in those vitamins. You didn't, did you?"

Asher sniffed. "Of course not. That witch doctor in St. Martin was responsible for the whole thing. I've been chained up for days now. Gives me an idea of what your restraints must feel like. I can't tell you how eager I am to have you at my mercy."

"Oh, you're a little randy tonight. We may have to up our play. Are you hungry, or would you rather get right to it?"

"Discipline first, dinner later."

****

Every light in the house was on when Asher swung onto his street in Tiburon. *What the hell is going on?* Would the government be stupid enough to search the house with all the lights on? If the housekeeper was dumb enough to let strangers in his house, he'd have her head. He turned off the main avenue of the estate community and onto his private drive. Only a few feet in, he was stopped by two armed guards standing in front of his high, wide security gate.

Asher rolled down the window of Tabby's Porsche with his most condescending scowl in place. "I'm the owner of this property. Why isn't my remote working, and who are you?"

"We're private security ordered by Mr. Albright. I'm sorry, sir, but there is a protective order against you. You're not allowed within one hundred and fifty yards of your wife or her property."

"That's impossible. I'm my wife's power of attorney."

The guard handed him court papers. "Not anymore, sir. I'm moonlighting on this job. I happen to be an officer in the San Francisco Police Department, and I'm advising you to take these papers, turn around at once, and consult your legal representative. You're not getting in here."

"We'll see about this!" Asher snapped, putting the car in reverse. He glanced over at Tabby, who was perusing the court order. "Can they do this?"

Tabby sighed. "Looks like they've done it. This is a protective order. You're locked out, Ash. You're barred from here and any other property Constance owns, including that software company." Tabby flipped through the papers, "It looks like Sam Albright has been given medical and financial power of attorney over her." She smoothed the documents and looked up to study his face. "Now you're getting tense again. Why don't we go to my place? You can release some of that anger, and afterward, we'll call your attorney."

Asher gave her a scathing look. "Let's see how much you can take tonight."

****

It was hard to make a hospital room cozy, but somehow, Sandy and the nurses managed. Everyone, including Jake, could see Cricket's spirits needed a little boost. Not only had she been through a great deal physically in the last week, but hearing her husband was intent upon killing her seemed to knock the emotional stuffing out of her.

They couldn't have real candles, that was a fire hazard, but they strung a line of fairy lights and placed artificial flickering votive candles on artful display. Ginger ale bubbled in plastic champagne flutes and easy on the stomach finger foods substituted as appetizers.

Cricket was showered, slathered with lotion, and dressed in a satin and lace shorty pajama set. Sandy washed and blew out her pixie haircut to give it a soft tousled look. She didn't want makeup, but a little blusher on pale cheeks and some light lipstick made her look almost like her old self. Cricket felt like a woman again, ready to snuggle with her man.

When they wheeled her back into her room, she noticed the rough hospital thermal blanket had been replaced with a light satin coverlet. Jake awaited her on the bed, leaning against a mountain of pillows covered with satin and lace. She gasped with delight.

"Hey, look at you, darlin'!" He opened his arms wide. "They didn't tell me they were turning your room into a spa. You look delicious enough to eat." He jumped up from the bed and scooped her out of the wheelchair. "You smell delicious too. I guess I shouldn't have skipped lunch." Cricket giggled as he thumped her playfully but gently onto the bed. "I hope they didn't wear you out with all the primping."

"I am delightfully exhausted. But it was so worth it!"

"The real you outshines any of the visions we've had in the past. Reality is so much better. Have some fake Champagne!"

"Are you trying to get me drunk on compliments and have your way with me, sir?"

"Oh, if only I could! We'll make a date for that, and the Champagne won't be fake!"

"Then let's cuddle, sugar!" She melted into his side. "What's over there?" She pointed at the silver tray of dietitian-approved snacks.

"It's a smorgasbord!"

They munched goodies and drank ginger ale as they chatted. Cricket put down her flute and entwined her fingers with Jake's.

"You don't think Asher was trying to kill me, do you?" She whispered in a small voice.

"I think…" Jake turned and kissed her softly, "you shouldn't worry about that right now."

She gave him an exasperated look. "I can't stop thinking about it, Jake. I want to discuss it. How would you feel if you found out someone you trusted was trying to kill you?"

Jake rubbed the bridge of his nose. "I'd feel pretty betrayed, and as if I couldn't trust my judgment, I guess." He looked at her thoughtfully. "I'm sorry we had to tell you. I know it was a horrible shock, but nothing is proven yet."

"Well, tetro…do…whatever…they found in the vitamins is a pretty good clue."

"Yeah, well, we don't know the whole story. The important thing is, there's a protective order against him. Parks is not allowed anywhere near you or your property, even if he knew where you were, which he doesn't…"

She played with their joined fingers. "And I'm divorcing him, right?"

"Well, as soon as you meet with your attorney and sign the papers. We didn't think it was right to wake you up from a coma and say, 'sign here'."

"No problem. Happy to sign. Never liked him anyway."

Jake gave her a sideways glance. "O…kay…why did you marry him?"

She shook her head. "Right now, I can't remember why. He certainly chased me with a single-minded intensity. It just sort of seemed like the thing to do. Worst mistake of my life."

"Do you feel safer because I resisted pursuing you?" He teased.

She gave him a skeptical look. "Didn't I hear you helped tear down a wall to get to me?"

He winked at her. "Well…"

"I've been thinking though," in her excitement Cricket rolled up on her knees to face him. "I never wanted to stay in San Francisco and do all this society/charity stuff. I mean," she shook her head and clarified. "I love supporting charities, don't get me wrong. I knew my family, and then Asher expected me to do that. It promoted our name and company."

"Yeah…" Jake nodded to keep her talking.

"Do you know, I usually wound up matching any donations we raised with those fancy events because they took so much out for expenses? The charities would have been left with almost nothing if I hadn't stepped in. If I never go to another charity ball, it'll be too soon for me."

Jake kissed her hands. "I'll bet you were the prettiest girl at the ball. But if you don't want to do that, what do you want to do?"

"I want to live somewhere magical with lots of land and lots of animals. I want to live somewhere peaceful. I want a place where nobody knows I'm a Nielson or cares how much money I have. I want a small town that has a real sense of community…"

"Do I get to live there, too?"

She gave him a flirty look. "It wouldn't be any fun without you!" She quieted. "Oh, but maybe that's not what you want. Do you want bright lights and a big city?"

Jake laughed. "Definitely not. I've been in the brightest lights and biggest cities. Do you know what those lights are made of? Gas and electricity. Illusion. I like your idea better."

"Do you like animals?"

"I love animals. I grew up in the country, you know. If it hadn't been for animals and spirit, I wouldn't have had anyone to talk to most of my childhood."

"You know Asher would never allow me to have pets. God forbid there should be a living creature that would take my attention from him. Where is he now, Jake? Because I'd like to greet him with a couple of big dogs when we get home."

"Big dogs, huh? Got it. I can make it happen." He chuckled. "Don't worry, though, we have big security guards standing post everywhere right now." He paused thoughtfully. "They're not as cute as big dogs, but I would give anything to have seen the look on Parks' face when they turned him away from the house tonight."

"What?" Her eyes grew huge, and her tone shattered the scale. "He tried to get in tonight?"

Jake chuckled. "Yep. While you were getting glamorous in the bathroom, the security team called. They sent ole' Asher packing. Wait till he finds out his Saville Row bespoke suits and all those stupid hats are waiting for him in a Pod warehouse."

Cricket gave a throaty laugh. "Oh, he will hate that! What about his gun collection? He has some rare and costly guns. What happened to them?"

Jake made a sad face. "You know, when someone has a protective order against them, the state of California confiscates all firearms and ammunition they own. Theoretically, those items are put away in police lock-up. It would be catastrophic if somehow the chain of possession was dropped, and they wound up lost."

Cricket laughed. "Oh, you better be careful. He'll come after you with a kitchen spatula!"

Jake put a modest hand over his chest. "Don't worry about me, ma'am. Me and my big dogs can handle him."

"Yes! Big dogs! When can we get them?"

Jake held her closer, "You want big sky, small town, lots of room for dogs to run?"

"Yeah."

"Sounds like Montana… but it's cold."

Cricket playfully shivered, "I don't like cold, and I don't ski. Go on…"

"Peaceful vibrations? Endless hiking paths and the best sunsets?"

Her eyes danced, "Take me there now!"

"Slow down, darlin', I need to find a realtor in Sedona, Arizona." His lips curled mischievously.

"Arizona? I have never been there. Tell me more…" She snuggled, waiting.

Jake caught her hand and kissed her palm. "Lots of good vibrations there. Do you need more info? Let me work on it."

Chapter 24

San Francisco, California

The night had never been so long. Tabitha ached everywhere. What didn't hurt from the actual 'discipline' was muscle pain from trying to get away. Asher was out of his mind with anger, and she dumped fuel on the fire by suggesting he "get your anger out" on her. An important lesson was that kind of encouragement didn't lessen anger; it increased it.

"Watermelon!" She screamed. "Watermelon! I can't take it anymore! Please!"

Asher's face twisted with rage. "Watermelon? Really? Are you bringing out your safe word? I thought you were made of tougher stuff. You can take more."

"No. I can't." She sobbed. "Please, Asher, watermelon!"

"What did you say?" His lips sneered down at her, his fingers twisted in her hair and tore away a chunk. "Less talking, do something else with that mouth."

She crabbed away from him. "No. I'm finished, we're done."

He lunged at her, "We're not done until I say we're done."

She inched herself up the wall to a standing position where she shook with fear. "I've used my safe word. If you won't honor it…" She steeled herself for his reaction. "You're going to have to leave…"

"Leave?" He roared. "Leave and go where, you stupid whore?"

"I don't care. Just get out!"

She cringed back as he swallowed the space between them in two long strides. Her head bounced off the wall with such force she barely remembered his kicks to her ribs or the arm he nearly broke when he dragged her to the front door to 'say goodbye'. If her condo neighbor hadn't banged on the door, would he have killed her? She didn't know. She slid into blessed oblivion for the next few hours.

****

The office for No Minimum LLC was in a mixed-use high rise in downtown San Francisco where Asher also maintained an efficiency unit as a playroom unknown to his tight-ass wife. Technically it was owned by his company, though Cricket's name was also on both leases. Surely they hadn't discovered the playroom…

It was still pre-dawn when he called for a cab to take him to the office. He was pissed that he had to wait fifteen minutes on the street. It made him too vulnerable to government surveillance.

Building security was always minimal at this time of day, and Asher was not surprised the doorman's post was vacant. He'd use his key card. He swiped it once and got a red light in return. With mounting agitation, he swiped two more times before the security guard showed up behind the double doors.

"Hey! My card isn't working, buddy, let me in."

The security guard gave him a cold stare. "Sorry, Mr. Parks, I've got a court order says you're no longer allowed in the building."

Asher raged. "Son of a bitch!" *Does that worthless guard have a smirk on his face?*

The guard continued. "You should know they cleaned out of your office and your little playroom. When they started dragging some of that stuff out, I thought you were opening a new Lowe's with all the chains and ropes and clamps and crap. Then, wow! You had stuff I sure never saw at Lowe's."

"Shut up, you nebbish!"

The guard gave him a satisfied grin. "Well, I may be a nebbish, but I'm a nebbish inside this building. I think you need to move along before I call the police. We don't need an early morning ruckus on my watch."

Asher turned his back on the man and put the phone to his ear to call another cab. "I need a lift to the airport." *Once I pick up my car at the airport, I'll drive directly to the docks.*

****

Cricket moved to the rehab center of the hospital and Jake was directed to honor visiting hours. The doctors felt it was vital Cricket learn anew to care for herself, and she couldn't do that if he provided constant support. As much as he resisted the idea of leaving her, he understood the rationale and was comforted by the fact that guards remained on her door.

"Not much to show for a month here." Paul joked when Jake neatly packed every item he'd stored at the Haight-Ashbury house into one suitcase. He moved into the Tiburon house today to supervise the cleanup, remove any remnant of Parks, and make sure all the equipment needed for rehab was in place.

Jake nodded. "I always said I travel light. Guess that'll change once Cricket gets a hold of me."

"You know women; they're not happy unless they're dressing us like paper dolls." Paul agreed.

Sandy laughed. "Cricket told me, she bought you a whole wardrobe of linen draw-string pants to show off your fine ass. That's a quote."

Jake looked behind him. "Thanks to martial arts, I do have a magnificent ass. And I've gotta take that phone away from her before there's no room left in the closet. Anyway," He opened his arms to both of them for hugs. "I can't say thanks enough. I could never have rescued her without your help. She should be going home soon, and we'll invite you guys over for toasted marshmallows on the patio."

Sandy grimaced. "Marshmallows, hell, I'm bringing chocolate and graham crackers too."

Jake gave her an appalled gasp. "Is that vegan?"

"Don't know, don't care."

****

Dr. Angela Franklin was a good friend and understood Tabby's kink. When Tabby eventually came to on the floor of her living room, she managed to get to the phone and call her.

"Don't worry about how you look or even about clothes. Throw on a raincoat, call an Uber, and get to my office." Angela instructed.

Tabby looked at her swollen face in the mirror. "Can't you come here?"

"Aside from having a waiting room full of patients, I need equipment to examine you. At a minimum I need X-rays, and if I need a CT scan, we have radiology in the building. So get yourself here, Tabby, or I'm calling an ambulance to take you to the hospital."

Tabby sighed. "Okay. I'll put on a coat, and I should be there in about fifteen minutes."

She was mostly numb during the ride over. The driver kept glancing at her in the rear-view mirror and suggested twice that he take her to an E.R. Angela had her staff alerted, and they whisked Tabby through a back door and into Angela's private office before she even got to the waiting room.

The X-rays of her fractured ribs were apparent even to Tabby's untrained eye. As Angela ran down the list of her injuries, Tabby sagged in her chair, her adrenaline flagging badly. "You have a concussion, fractured ribs on your left side, and a torn triceps tendon in your right arm." Tabby groaned. "If you were anyone else, I'd admit you and call the police. But Tabby, you know better than I what that would entail. You'd receive negative publicity, and your reception at the D.A.'s office would be even worse. Plus, that nut Asher would be arrested, you'd have to testify…"

Tabby waved her to a stop. "I know. I'm just gonna change my locks, change my number and have him barred from my building."

"Probably the best course of action. Meanwhile, you're staying with me tonight, and if I don't like the way you look in the morning, you're coming back to the office with me."

Tabby groaned again. "When can I go back to work? And what am I gonna tell them?"

The two women were quiet, thinking. "Why don't we say you were in an auto accident? Your injuries are consistent with that, and I can write you off work for as long as we need." Angela wrote some things on her chart and turned. "I have a friend who could inflict some damage on dear Asher if you want."

Tabby's eyes opened wide. "I do not want that. Besides the fact that two wrongs don't make a right, Asher would be just the kind of guy to suspect I arranged it and have me hauled in. I think ignoring him is the wisest choice."

Chapter 25

Cricket broke into a hot sweat which she welcomed as a sign of exertion. She felt a drop trickle down her face and plop onto her physical therapist's arm. He looked at her in alarm.

"You okay, Cricket?"

"I'm fine, Jerry. Stop treating me like an invalid." She wiped more sweat off her forehead with her arm.

The fiftyish man with the solid build and kind blue eyes narrowed those eyes at her now. "I'm not against hard work, young lady, but if you work too hard, you're gonna undo progress. So take it easy." He moved her right hand from the parallel bar down to her side. "Since you seem to be balancing well with two legs and one hand, let's watch you walk the length of the parallel bars with one arm at your side."

Cricket took a deep breath, nodded, and made it all the way to the end without faltering. She turned to face him, a hot flush suffusing her pallor. "How's that?"

"That is outstanding. Now, let's sit you down, have a little water, give it a rest."

"I don't wanna rest. In fact, why am I only doing therapy once a day? Why can't it be twice a day?"

Jerry studied her. "You know, there's a reason for every exercise and rest period. I know you're anxious to get better. And I'm not saying we can't do some gentle exercises in the afternoons. I'm happy to ask Dr. Clark for an order. But I'm not going to let you exhaust yourself so you can be a hundred percent for your young man."

"Well, you sexist! What makes you think I'm doing this for Jake? I'm working on getting myself well."

Jerry gave her a disbelieving look. "Cricket, I have five daughters. Yeah, I'm sure you are working on getting yourself well. And it just happens to be an added bonus that you'll be on your feet for Jake, right?"

"Well, maybe." She admitted.

"So get on your feet again. You have stairs to climb."

"Slave driver."

****

Jake drove by the Tiburon house once before and found it daunting. That glimpse in no way prepared him for the splendor inside. Von met him at the gate and began the tour.

"That car in the driveway," Von pointed to a late model Bentley sedan, "will be yours until you choose another." Jake raised a brow. "Hey, don't give me that look. These are Cricket's orders. She says if you resist, I should tell you it was her dad's car. It's sentimental."

Jake pointed at his road-worn 2005 Mercedes. "I have a car."

Von gave him a doubtful look. "Make the lady happy, Jake."

Jake grinned. "I intend to. In my car. Though I'm sure we'll find a way to honor her dad with this one. She can drive it when they give her the okay."

"Oh, I see," Von observed. "You're drawing boundaries around her money versus your money."

Jake shrugged. "I don't need her money. I have money of my own. Not as much as she does, but as much as I need, thanks. My biggest worry right now is how to complete the six hours I need on my degree."

"You're resourceful. You'll work it out."

Von showed Jake the interior of the house and explained that new housekeepers had been hired to start tomorrow. "Cricket can have her folks back if she wants, but for right now, we wanna make sure no one with any loyalties to Parks is on this property. We figured it would be safest to hire new domestic staff."

"Whatever you think. How about safety on the grounds?"

Von pointed to the various areas of weakness on the property. "We've trimmed back the landscaping significantly. I'm sure Cricket won't be too pleased by that, but we need to see what's around us. Short of an attack by drone, I don't see anyone getting to her."

Jake searched through the kitchen cabinets until he found glasses and water for the two of them. "You know, Cricket loves animals, and I guess Parks would never let her have any." Von nodded. "Plus, I think she has some jitters about coming out of the safety of the hospital and back home. Though God knows, they're practically barring the door to keep her in at this point."

Von laughed. "Yeah, she doesn't strike me as a lady who stays down for long. So, animals go on. Not a lot of room for animals around here."

"She would really like a couple of guard dogs." Jake laughed, "As she put it, *big* dogs. You have any connections for protection dogs?"

Von nodded. "Now, Jake, you know I'm gonna tell you yes. As a matter of fact, I have a Ranger buddy who handled dogs in the service. When he retired, he opened a training facility and kennel. He's the best."

"Can we get him here with a couple of dogs, so we'll have them in place when Cricket's ready to go home?"

"You bet. Let me make a call and see what he suggests."

Jake grinned hugely. "Great, and there's just one more thing I'd like you to ask about…"

****

Asher idled along the dock at Gable Island. The only pieces of property not in Cricket's name were his boat and this godforsaken island. He sounded the ship's horn in impatient blasts to let the island caretaker know he needed assistance. After two minutes, no one appeared. He blasted again, leaning on the horn angrily. *Nothing. I guess that nasty message from my lawyer meant I have no staff left.* He glanced up at the unseen watchers in the sky. *I've gotta get out of sight.*

When none of the lights went on, and no one ran to assist him, like the truculent child he was, Asher stalked around the boat to grab the mooring line. Cursing with each movement, he fastened the line and then jogged up the dock to take the steps up to the house two at a time.

The path usually swept clean and tidy was strewn with leaves and debris. The house was dark, and Cricket's bedroom window curtain blew out lazily in the gray dawn breeze. A shiver and a tentacle of fear crawled up his back. It was beginning to sink in that Asher's world had changed. *They're closing in.*

He had to use his key to access the locked-up house. The servants were gone, but how? *Were they rounded up by the CIA? If so, what did they tell the government? Were they the reason for the protective order against him? Is that why my attorney sent that snarky note?* He'd fire the S.O.B.

He clamored down the basement stairs to the saferoom and gasped when he saw the massive hole exploded in the wall. He'd suspected it, but now he knew for sure. *They have her. She's one of them now.*

Asher checked the kitchen. He hadn't eaten since yesterday afternoon because after their 'play' Tabby seemed in no mood to cook. He clicked on the light. There wasn't much in the refrigerator, a hunk of cheese, some outdated milk, didn't these Brazilians believe in boxed dinners? There was plenty of flour, sugar, butter, and the like, but no ready-to-cook items. The best he could find was stale crackers and a tin of sardines. It would have to do until he could get some sleep and head to the marina for food.

First, he needed to secure his cash. Asher headed for the lighthouse. He pulled the skeleton key from his jacket pocket but found it unnecessary. The door hung by one hinge after the troops kicked it in. He imagined the Coast Guard were in more of a hurry to usher Cricket and the Brazilians to San Francisco proper than to search for his money.

Asher shouldered open the door and went directly to the brick he'd spent hours digging away from its fellows. Behind it sat a waterproof packet containing twenty thousand dollars in hundred-dollar bills.

On the way back to the house, he stood in an open area and tried his attorney again. No answer, not even an invitation to voice mail. The call clicked off. *Oh, he is so fired.* Well, it should be no great hardship to find another attorney to help him get his passport back. Once he had that, he'd take off for his money in Switzerland and then a pleasant life somewhere the CIA couldn't get to him.

Let Cricket rot in some fancy nursing home somewhere. She would die eventually, and since they were still married, the bulk of the estate, what wasn't depleted by the needless care, would come to him. He'd have to check with Dr. Baptiste to see how long he thought she had if nature took its course.

It was all a waiting game. Asher would stay either in the island house or on his boat for the next week or so until the problems with his passport were corrected. This morning he'd grab a couple of hours sleep, and then shower and shave and make himself presentable.

He'd stock the Sea Ray up with a week's food, buy himself some clothes, since he couldn't get into his house, and hire a new attorney. He needed someone who gave him the respect he deserved. The attorney could help him find out where Cricket was. *Yeah, I need to know where Cricket is.*

****

Asher stocked his wallet with more than his usual thousand dollars in cash, which was a good thing. He stood in the check-out line with over two hundred dollars' worth of groceries, and his credit card was inexplicably declined. He used his black Amex card at Cable Car Clothier's, and the salesman destroyed it with seeming glee. He still purchased his items with cash, but of course, his reputation was ruined, no matter his protest that his credit was pristine.

As soon as he got to the boat and charged his phone, someone was getting a furious call. *Heads will roll!*

180

Chapter 26

That night, Jake clicked on the flickering votive candles and turned off the overhead lights. He and Cricket requested no interruptions for an hour. "God knows what the nurses think." He teased Cricket, who blushed furiously. "You'd be more embarrassed if they walked in on us."

"What's up your sleeve, you bad boy?" She demanded with a wicked grin.

"Don't get all hot and bothered." He kissed along the graceful column of her neck and then backed away. "I was meditating about how to help you last night, and this meditation was given to me."

"Oh? The other side is eager for romance?"

"Not romance. Get yourself settled in your recliner. I have a meditation for you."

"I like my idea better…"

"Mmm. I can't wait to entertain it myself, but this one is about healing."

Cricket pouted prettily and readjusted the pillow behind her back. "Okay. Shoot."

She closed her eyes, and Jake started the induction, instructing her to float with him down a staircase of clouds until they reached a carved-stone wall. She was instructed to push on the wall to pivot it, and they found themselves in a 'temple of healing'.

"What is this place? It's noticeably ancient..." She whispered and was interrupted by a tall being radiating light. He? She? Male energy seemed to glow from him.

"What does thee wish?" The being asked pleasantly.

"I – what?" She stammered.

"What does thee wish?"

Cricket glanced uncertainly at Jake, who nodded encouragement. "I've come for healing. I've been...ill..." She finished lamely.

The being's entire focus was upon her from her crown to her toes and back again. She felt as if she was being scanned. *Is he human? Some kind of android?*

The being's laugh echoed around the room. "I am not unlike thee except I have occupied this healing center for eons, and thou hast come and gone as thou had the need."

"So...I've been here before?" Cricket looked around now, noting the age of the stone walls and tiles beneath her feet. "It certainly doesn't look like a modern healing center, does it?"

"Wouldst thou feel more as if healing was accomplished within these walls if I did this?" The being waved his arm and the moss-covered ancient walls became clean drywall, painted the institutional green and beige of the average medical center. Neatly lettered signs pointed them to 'Diagnostics', 'Treatment Rooms', and 'Post Evaluation'.

Cricket glanced distractedly back to their greeter. "I'd like whatever form you feel is most comfortable. I thought the stone walls and tiles and carved signage was very quaint and comforting."

"As thee wishes." Their greeter waved an arm again, and they were back in the ancient healing center. "Poison, I see, hast been the culprit in thy illness." His stare bore into her. "Not only poison but accompanied by a curse." He tsked. "Much has been done to heal thy body. Now, we must heal thy mind, thy spirit, and thy soul."

Cricket laid a tentative hand on his forearm, feeling suddenly dizzy from the power that emanated from him. "How do we do that?"

"Let thy emotions be at peace, child. It is not as onerous as thou thinkst." His pat on her hand was immediately comforting. "Come dear one; thou wilt enter the room of discernment, where we will assist thee to remember who thou truly art."

"You will?"

"Yes. All who seek healing have only to remember who they truly are. That is how all healing begins."

"It is?"

"Yes."

"But that's so simple."

"Simple and yet difficult to do when thou must fight the illusions of your mortal world." The being of light grinned at her. "Have no fear. All will be well." He pushed against a stone in the wall, and a doorway slid open to reveal an Egyptian looking slab with a stone neck rest. "Please settle thyself upon the bed, and I will return as soon as I've seen to thy companion."

He didn't seem like a guy you could argue with, so Cricket buried her sense of unfamiliarity and did as she was told.

Immediately, different colored lights, rose, yellow, blue, and green began to scan her body, and she soon drifted into a light trance state.

****

The being of light gestured Jake along. "And now for thee, young man…"

"Me? Why me? I'm not sick."

"No, the trauma has not yet translated itself from thy aura to thy body to induce illness. We intend to see that does not happen." He scanned Jake from crown to toe and back, as he had Cricket. "Thou hast been the hero in this tale, has thou not?"

"Er…" Jake frowned.

"Thou hast been a brave defender and have not admitted to thyself the emotional trauma and fear thou hast endured." Jake squirmed uncomfortably. "We will help divest thee of the fear, clear the emotional body, and keep thee strong and healthy for thy love." He pushed at a stone panel in the wall, and once again, a doorway swung open. He pointed at the stone slab with the neck rest. "Settle thyself and be at peace."

****

The sole question coming to Cricket's mind was, *How do I heal myself?*

The answer came back clearly. "Thou must decide to do it."

Well, that's just ridiculous! Cricket thought irritably. *If it were that simple, people would be healed every day.*

"People are healed every day."

I know, but I mean —

"People *are* healed every day. Those who are not have differing problems. For thee, it is a decision. Wilt thou be healed?"

"Yes!" Her answer was emphatic and emotional, and suddenly, she could see herself in the perfection from which she was created. Cricket gasped at the beauty of it – of her. From that moment, honoring that experience, she knew she began to heal.

****

Jake, too, experienced the differing colored lights. "Thou art filled with worry." The disembodied voice spoke directly to his mind.

"I wish I weren't, but there's still a lot to worry about."

"Art thou a creator?"

"Of some things."

The voice laughed. "Well said. Thou art a creator. And dost thou care for thy creations?"

"I guess so..." Jake answered uncertainly.

"Dost thou believe the universe was made by a Creator?"

"Yes."

"Then dost thou believe the Creator maintains His creations? As thou maintains thine?"

"Maybe. I mean, I guess so."

"And dost the Creator need thy help to maintain His creations?"

"I suppose not. I was told if He needs my help He'll say so."

"Then, why worry? The creator hast made and is maintaining thee, perfect and pure as the creation in His mind. What else is there?"

"I..." Jake was stumped. "Nothing...I guess..." Jake knew this concept would take some serious thought.

"Then worry for nothing, for the Creator is worried for nothing."

****

When Jake came out of the meditation, he found Cricket awake and watching him. "Do you remember that place? I mean, remember it from before?"

"Vaguely. Except, when I saw it before, eons ago, it was all bright and shiny new."

She nodded. "I know. Does it sound crazy to say we were there in Atlantis? That it was a healing center in Atlantis?"

Jake grinned and pulled her into an encompassing hug, rocking her back and forth as they embraced. "It doesn't sound any crazier than anything else we've been through these past few months. I say if there are ancient memories of Atlantis, there must be a reason for them."

Cricket turned her face up for a kiss. "How cool was that?"

Chapter 27

The next morning Cricket stood in the bathroom without a walker, brushing her teeth, a choice about which she knew the nurses would disapprove. She heard Jake's 'shave and a haircut' knock, and the door to her room opened. "Anybody home?" He called.

"In here." She garbled with a mouthful of toothpaste, rinsed, wiped her mouth, and walked out to meet him. "Hi!"

"You look different today. What's different?" He studied her. "No limp?"

"Nope!"

"No walker?" She stood solidly, unsupported, on her own two feet and nothing more. "Wow, darlin'! That's great!" Something wiggled inside his jacket and whined plaintively.

"You *sound* different today." She teased. "How long have you been whining?"

Jake shut the door carefully and unzipped his jacket. An appealing black furry face, with dark soulful eyes and cream brows and cheeks, peered hesitantly out at her. The puppy's long pointed ears drooped adorably, one on its forehead, and one to the side.

"Aw!" Cricket melted with love on the spot. "Who's this?" She lifted the puppy out of Jake's arms to cuddle it to her chest. "Boy? Girl?"

"Girl," Jake said, watching the two of them bond with great satisfaction. "Her mom and dad are outside waiting for her with their trainer."

"I see." Cricket sat the puppy on the bed where she joined her. "Oh, Jake! She's adorable."

"Yeah, she's pretty cute. I thought maybe you'd enjoy her hanging around while mom and dad patrolled the house." He scratched the puppy behind her ears, and she leaned into him, obviously enjoying the attention.

"Wow, she's perfect, isn't she?" Cricket exclaimed, looking the baby over. "Look at that gorgeous coat! Black and tan and cream, the perfect markings for a Shepherd! And look at the size of those paws -- big as dinner plates! She's gonna be a big girl. Aren't you sweetie?" The puppy charged her to lick her face. "Aren't you the sweetest thing?" Cricket cuddled her.

"Her mom and dad are waiting down there. Wanna see them?" Jake pointed to the window.

"Sure."

"They're protection trained, and they'll begin guarding the house after you come home. Their trainer said you should have a little settle-in time first because he's gotta teach us their commands and all that."

"Oh, that's great. I mean, it's nice to have protection and all, but I'll love having dogs around the place again." She looked out the window and saw a young man with military bearing holding the leashes of two spectacular German Shepherds, one on each side of him.

"I think they ought to provide entertainment and protection, don't you?" Jake laughed. "And of course, this little one has to come too. She'll be the most entertaining of them all."

Cricket waved at the trainer and giggled. "I think we're gonna need a bigger house!" The puppy looked up at her and whined again. "Oh, I think someone's missing her mom." The puppy licked her face.

"Yeah, she probably needs to go back down. She's only six weeks, barely old enough to be gone from mom for even a little while. What are you gonna call her?"

Cricket held the puppy at arm's length to study her little face, then drew her close to her body again. "See the way those eyes sparkle? What are Mom and Dad called?"

"Hansel and Gretel."

"Oh. I suppose she should have a German name like Heidi or something, but I like Sparkle. Doesn't she look like a Sparkle to you?"

"Absolutely." The puppy began to escalate from a whimper to anxious yips.

"Uh, oh. You'd better take Sparkle back down to her mom before we get scolded. Besides, I have to go to physical therapy. You're coming back for the treatment team meeting this afternoon, right?"

"You bet." He reached out for the puppy. "C'mon, Sparkle. Your momma's waitin' for you."

****

Asher sat stony-faced starring down the thousand dollar an hour attorney. This was the third guy with whom he'd had this fruitless conversation, and his frustration escalated far above rage on the verge of violence.

"You are a poor risk, Mr. Parks." The attorney said in the same high-and-mighty tone Asher reserved for the working classes – attorneys, doctors, and accountants. "You are under investigation by Homeland Security for bringing a restricted substance into the country. There is a protective order against you because the police found that same substance in vitamins you were giving to your wife. In fact, allegedly, to hide your crime, you took your wife out of legitimate medical care and housed her on an island with unlicensed caregivers. I would not be surprised if you're brought up on charges for attempted murder. The IRS has frozen all your accounts because of suspected fraud and tax evasion. Homeland Security will never release your passport under these conditions. The chances of you being able to pay for our services is slim to none." The man waved a dismissive hand at Asher. "Might I suggest you try Legal Aid?"

Asher's entire body shook with fury when he shot out of his seat. "Let me tell you something, Mr. smug attorney. You've been trying to get into the Marin Country Club for years. I hold the deciding vote. Do you think that will ever happen now? Might I suggest Sausalito's Putt-Putt Heaven? I'll find someone to help me out of this situation, and when I do, all of you condescending bastards will pay. No one has ever been so unfairly treated by the legal system!"

"Uh-huh. Well, good luck with that, Mr. Parks. Now, I'm afraid I have another client waiting. Sarah will meet you at her desk with your receipt for our consultation fee."

Asher blasted out of the office and blew past Sarah like a tropical cyclone. He pounded his fists on the brass elevator doors in utter impotent madness. Slowly, a devious smile appeared. He pulled his cell from his suit pocket and dialed.

"Tabitha Daniels, please." He said in a strangled tone striving for pleasant. "What do you mean she's out of the office, she's just back from vacation!" He stared incredulously at the phone. "Auto accident? Fine!" He ended the call and redialed. There was a high-pitched tone and then, "This number is not accepting calls at this time. Message 74122."

She's blocking me! That stupid whore. She can't refuse me. This is all Connie's fault; Connie and her stupid cousin Sam.

Chapter 28

Jake had never totally appreciated how quickly the human body rebuilds itself when given appropriate care. He knew their unconventional therapy in the Atlantis healing center had much to do with Cricket's rapid recovery. More than that, she was steadily gaining weight and no longer the wasted waif she'd been when they arrived at the hospital. She began complaining about the food, which the nurses assured him was a good sign.

Today, Cricket preceded all of them into the main conference room, sans walker or cane, to discuss her progress. *She's moving pretty fast. How long will it be before she's running?*

Cricket turned to Dr. Clark. "You draw labs on me daily, you do weekly EEGs, and someone is always taking me down to radiology. Let me ask you; it's been twenty-one days since I woke up. Have you seen any real change in any of that testing within the last week?"

Dr. Clark's eyes twinkled. "I have a feeling you're driving at something here, Cricket."

She gave him an exasperated look. "Yeah. I wanna know what more this hospital can do for me? I mean, I owe all of you my life, and I'm very grateful, but I'm thinking if all the tests are normal now, I wanna go home."

Dr. Clark nodded. "Perfectly understandable request. And, to answer your question, yes, your testing is back to normal levels. Nothing we couldn't monitor with routine testing from home. But…

Cricket scowled. "Oh, here it comes."

"But," Dr. Clark continued calmly. "You haven't finished your rehab therapy, and you have a way to go on that. Although I will admit your progress in the past week has been remarkable, you still need work on balance and core strengthening."

Jake cleared his throat. "I've been looking into that, Doc, and you know, Cricket has considerable resources. I know we can hire full-time therapists and equipment to help her do all her rehab at home. When she gets to the point where they want equipment that perhaps they can't furnish at home, she can always do outpatient rehab."

Cricket turned violet eyes, bright with unshed tears, on the doctor. "Please, Dr. Clark? Please! You can't imagine how much I want to go home."

Clark considered for a moment, tapping his pen on a pad of paper. "Okay." He decided slowly. "But…"

"Another but," Cricket complained.

"But, you have to come for weekly checkups. We're not going to have you backslide just because you're eager to go home."

"I promise! I promise! Please! Can we do all this today? I want to be home before the weekend."

"Alright." Dr. Clark agreed. "I'll write orders." He looked at Jake. "Get ready for a flurry of activity. And don't you have some legal problems you need to settle?"

"Yes," Jake agreed, "Nothing we can't do at home."

****

Cricket hugged herself trying to contain the thrill of being back in her own home after months away. She couldn't see any remnant of Asher Parks. Jake and Sam must have worked together to eliminate any vestige of him left behind. The Tiburon house was all hers now, and she loved it at the same time she longed to be free of it. Cricket wanted to get away from this house, Asher Parks and San Francisco. She wasn't exaggerating one bit when she told Jake she wanted a small town, peace, and anonymity.

Navigating long distances still required rest, and she was disappointed that she was wearied by the hubbub of being discharged. It was a long car trip from Palo Alto to Tiburon, but she didn't expect it to be so exhausting. Here she was, finally, finally, walking into her own home on her own two feet. She walked up to the wall of windows in the great room and sighed deeply, admiring the gorgeous view of the bay and skyscrapers of San Francisco far in the distance. It was beautiful, but Cricket felt uneasy here all the same.

What if I ask Jake to take us out of here and check us into a hotel? Cricket dismissed the idea as impractical. They needed to set up rehab equipment. There would be medical personnel, not to mention domestic staff going in and out all the time. The many stairs in the house would be both daunting and therapeutic, only

195

an inconvenience, really. She needed to suck it up, put on a happy face, and tell them all how very ecstatic she was to be home.

****

On her first night home, Cricket was too exhausted to even take a pre-bed shower. Oh, but lying next to Jake, sleeping in his arms, was heaven. Despite her protests, he was up and out of bed before her, greeting therapists and the medical equipment company. What a change from Asher who never considered anyone's needs but his own.

****

The day was pleasantly tiring, and Cricket retreated to the teakwood deck outside her bedroom. She watched the ships and listened to the music of their horns. Always before when she watched the bay, she thought of the delightful adventures awaiting the occupants of those ships.

The gauntlet of the past months had significantly changed her outlook. Her husband secreted her onto his Sea Ray and transported her into the hands of strangers. These outsiders, under threat of being returned to their native country, trusted only their employer. They ignored their medical oaths to do no harm and dutifully loaded poison into her tube feedings.

Did the Coast Guard make safety checks on small out of the way islands? Maybe the Coast Guard would have found her. Perhaps not. She wasn't afraid to die, but what a horrible way to go about it, poisoned by your husband and left to die with strangers.

Cricket was profoundly shaken by the story of the tetrodotoxin. Even though Jake tried to soften the blow, she knew Asher ordered it. It wasn't a mistake or an accident. She knew the man. It was an intentional attempt on her life.

Something no one mentioned was the car wreck. Yeah, she was angry and driving a little fast that day, but she was far from reckless. Not only that, but she'd had the car serviced earlier that week. It was in perfect shape. She dodged a bottle thrown by the car ahead of her, hit a pothole, and suddenly the car went out of control? She precisely remembered the moment when turning the steering wheel failed to correct her course. If she hadn't been thrown out, she would have died horribly in the consuming fire. This was Asher's dark hand, not rotten luck.

Her divorce attorney was due later in the week. Was it wrong that she not only wanted Asher in prison, she wanted everything he owned? Not for herself. She'd give the money to charity. She had more than enough. She wanted him divorced from every avenue of aid. *Let's see how he likes it.* She felt guilty. A spiritual person was supposed to be above such vindictiveness. *Well, I guess I need to evolve a little further because he's going to meet a buzz saw when he sees me again.*

Chapter 29

Marin County, California

Cricket designed and started the build on the house while she and Asher were still dating. When it was built, Cricket made sure the soaker tub in the master bath overlooked the harbor and was big enough for two. She and Asher never used it together. By the time the house was finished, she didn't want him in her bathtub.

Tonight, with mounting excitement, Cricket lit deliciously scented candles, played soft music through the sound system, and placed a lovely bottle of Champagne to chill in an ice bucket along with two elegant flutes.

The water temperature was perfect, and there were opalescent bubbles piled up in the water. Cricket turned out the overhead light, dropped her robe, and stepped into the tub. She could hear Jake in the bedroom, hanging his clothes in the closet.

"Sugar?" She called. "I dropped my washcloth on the floor. Could you come in and get it for me?"

Jake laughed at her. "What? Did it grow feet?" He opened the door and wearing only a robe and a smile, peeked around it. "Whoa! What's on *your* mind, darlin'?" He sauntered in to pick up the washcloth and dangled it at her.

She gave him a saucy grin. "Will you wash my back?"

His return grin was smirkingly cute. "I'll even wash your front!"

"You know, this is a huge tub. It was built for two…"

"We wouldn't want to disappoint the builders." He dropped his robe.

Cricket saw his fabulous body many times on the astral plane. In this flickering candlelight, Jake exuded both his athletic physicality and his splendid intentions to worship her body with every sense. Jake's physique was lean perfection, with smooth skin drawn tightly over muscles well-defined at every angle. Her index finger reached of its own volition to draw down his treasure trail. He stepped into the tub, and with athletic grace, settled at the opposite end, his arms reaching for her. She stared, mesmerized by his quirky, crooked grin and the dusting of hair on his muscled chest that caught some bubbles when he sat back...

"…Darlin'?"

She blinked back into focus. "Sorry. What?"

"I said, is this Champagne for us?"

"Unless the mice intend to drink it, I think it is."

He patted the porcelain of the tub and grinned down at her. "This is real! I keep waiting for everything to disappear…"

Cricket leaned forward and playfully bit up his neck to his ear, and over to his perfect lips. She smiled into the kiss. "It's real, sugar. You and I are real!"

Jake's hands explored the hollows of her body that were becoming curves again. He caught her knees and pulled her up the length of his legs. "You feel real to me!" His hands roamed to her backside, and he squeezed both cheeks as she straddled him.

She laughed and squealed as her hand embraced his proud erection. *He feels even more potent in the flesh!* Her heart pounded when the throbbing in her hand answered her caress. She gasped. "This feels really fine too!"

Their lips caught each other in a furtive fire. Jake groaned. "C'mere, darlin', I have just the spot for you!" He slid her over his waking flesh and pulled her knees tighter around his waist.

"Ooh! I like this spot!" Dissolving into a passionate kiss again, they escalated their mutual explorations of earthly flesh. Cricket sighed with the thrill of him beneath her. She'd had a revelry of enjoying Jake on the astral plane, but this was flesh and blood and hot. She looked forward to expressing and receiving love like this forever.

Jake filled her body as his love filled her soul. Poetic and sweet movements began as they kissed and nipped each other playfully. Sublime moments escalated to driving passion. Cricket's head fell back as she panted toward completion. She gasped in delighted surprise as her body held him with sacred friction. A ragged moan, breathy and deep, escaped her moments before she felt his body quiver, tighten and release. A jaw clenching groan emerged between them as he caught her to him in a desperate kiss.

After several seconds, he released her, and they rested sweetly in each other's arms. She loved the feel of him against her as the bubbles swirled around them. A few moments later, she giggled contagiously.

Jake put a finger under her chin to draw her face up. "What's so funny?"

"Would you mind doing that again, please?"

He threw his head back and barked out a laugh. "Give me a few, and I'll see what I can do."

****

They cuddled in a whirl of silky sheets, their spirits dancing on clouds of physical exhaustion. Cricket lay against his chest, listening to the calm, steady beat of his heart. "You know what I think we should do?" She murmured.

"I can't right now." He admitted with a chuckle.

"No, that would be lovely, but I was going to say, I think we should have a little thank you party this weekend. You know, we could invite everyone who had anything to do with helping us. Sam and Sandy and Paul and Barry, of course, all the doctors and nurses and therapists, and Coast Guard, everyone. Everyone who helped."

Jake tilted his head down. "That's a lot of people, darlin'."

She shrugged. "It's a big house. There's plenty of room; we could cater a bar-b-que. We have a huge staff; they're invited too. I mean, what good is it having all these people working for us if we can't have a good time together?"

Jake laughed. "Okay. If you feel up to it, I say let's do it. I'll drop off invitations personally."

She laughed. "This'll be so much fun!"

Jake tousled her short hair; his tone suggestive. "You know what I think we should do?"

"What?"

"I'll show you…"

Chapter 30

Santa Clara, California

Sam Albright stopped by the office on Saturday morning, as was his routine. It was probably silly, but he liked the quiet of being one of the few workers there on the weekend. He could concentrate without interruption, and he used the time to "put the company to bed for the weekend."

With the threat of Parks out of the way, Sam was free to recruit more business, and interest was increasing daily. He considered putting the company up for an IPO, and that would mean hours of overtime in the coming weeks.

Cricket was open to him purchasing the majority share if he wanted. She wanted out, and he couldn't blame her. The divorce and criminal charges against Parks were yet to be sorted out. She had rehab and a new relationship with Jake. She had enough on her plate.

He and Jake had quietly determined not to mention anything about the suspicions that Parks had murdered not only his parents but hers. If something came of that, they'd sit her down in the gentlest possible way and tell her. *God, what a horrendous conversation that will be!*

Today was a day of celebration. Cricket was home from the hospital and doing well. This afternoon the bar-b-que celebration would lighten everyone's hearts. Sam looked forward to getting there a little early and helping with the setup, though he was sure she, Jake and the house staff had things well under control. He'd beefed up security a bit, to be sure everything was as safe as possible, and it would be great to relax with some steak and wine and chat.

He headed toward his car, his mind on the case of 1858 Cabernet Sauvignon Paso Robles secured in his trunk. It was his contribution to the celebration, though Cricket had sternly warned no homecoming gifts were expected. He grinned. *It's one of her favorites. She'll love it! I hope the doctors will let her have wine.*

Sam barely had time to settle himself behind the wheel when a petite redhead appeared in front of him in the parking lot. She fell to the ground holding her leg and crying. "Help me!" Her face crumpled in agony. "Oh, please, I think I broke my leg. Please help me!"

Sam leapt out of the car to run to her aid. When he was several yards away from his car, but only feet from her, a massive explosion behind him shook the ground. He threw his body over the woman's and held up an arm for cover as he turned to look behind him. Flames shot from his car and soared several feet into the air. He stared in shock and horror.

In another moment, he came to his senses and turned to look at the woman under him. "Are you alright…" he began, and then gaped at the empty pavement beneath him. She was gone. He scrambled to his knees and visually searched the almost vacant parking lot. He saw no one. *She had a broken leg. She couldn't have made it to a parked car…* What few employees were there stood outside the front doors, and two of the programmers ran to his side. Sirens screamed down the street, and a ladder truck followed by an ambulance and police vehicle roared to a stop by his flaming car.

The police and ambulance attendants pronounced him beyond lucky. One guy encouraged him to buy a lottery ticket. He had only scrapes and bruises from where he'd fallen on the girl. *The girl who wasn't there.*

He tried to tell the paramedic about the disappearing woman. After a search of the three other cars in the lot, and the perimeter of the building, he'd been assured it was probably a traumatic hallucination. "Are you sure you didn't hit your head when you fell, sir? Maybe we should take you to the hospital for a CT?"

Sam was jovial when he agreed what he saw was probably a result of the trauma. And no, he didn't need to go to the hospital. But he knew what he'd seen. The redhead, whoever she was, saved his life and vanished. *Wow. Maybe Jake can explain it.*

****

Asher Parks, watching with binoculars from the upper floor of the Hyatt Santa Clara down the street, wanted to scream with frustration. *What does it take to kill the damn Nielson family? Dean and Kathy went easily enough, but Cricket and Sam just won't fucking die! Why the hell did he leap from his car like that? He couldn't have known about the bomb. What the hell is going on?*

****

Stepping from the dock onto his boat, Asher still smarted under a sense of defeat. He should have taken care of Sam and then moved on to Cricket with no impediments. He was thwarted, and that only served to increase his paranoia. He threw the makings of a sandwich onto the counter of the boat's galley.

Paying no particular attention to what he stuffed between the pieces of bread, Asher's focus was riveted on the noon-time news.

The anchorman ended with the most tedious item of the day. "The CIA announced an audit of the environmental review of the Safe Drinking Water Act of 1974 and its relationship to the National Environmental Policy Act. The U.N. Secretary-General said in a statement, "No issue is of greater global importance than safe drinking water.""

Asher began the rapid eye blinking that was his precursor to a full-blown psychotic break. He incorporated any mention of the CIA into his delusions now. *The cat's out of the bag. They all know about me. Soon the Nielsons will use their power to have me dumped in a black-ops jail and forgotten.*

Asher stared at the television as the newscaster spoke directly to him through the camera. "In time, the entire population will be unable to tell reality from illusion. It's up to you now, Parks. You're the only one who can stop Cricket and her cousin."

Asher's sandwich fell into his lap as his thoughts jumped manically from subject to subject. He had to find a way to get to Cricket first. Killing her with his own two hands would be a pleasure now. He fingered the leather scabbard of his boning knife. He'd stab her – *multiple thrusts into her heart and gut ought to do the job. Or I could slice her throat. Yeah, yeah, that's even better, it will cut her vocal cords, and she can't cry out. If that nosy boyfriend of hers tries to interfere, I'll snap his spine at the neck.*

Time is slipping away. The government is closing in. They can take my freedom at any moment. "You have to move tonight." The newscaster told him irritably. *Yes. It has to be tonight.*

Chapter 31

Marin County, California

A patrolman was kind enough to take Sam home after they collected his statement and evidence. He needed to shower, patch himself up, and change clothes. He'd take the Beetle over to Cricket's, and she would have to settle for a nice case of Dos Equis. His gift of vintage Cabernet Sauvignon was now vintage lighter fluid in his immolated trunk. He pulled into the Tiburon circular drive a good two hours late and tossed the keys to the valet hired for the occasion.

****

Jake looked up from breaking ice bags into tubs of beer when Sam strolled in with his case. "Hey! Thought you got caught in Saturday beach traffic." He spotted the beer. "Dos Equis! I occasionally have a bit of that good stuff."

Sam gave a little wince as he walked from the great room down a step to the lower level of the kitchen. "Yeah, it's my favorite too. Sorry, I'm late…" He surveyed the bustling kitchen. "Could you and I grab Von and have a little talk outside?"

Jake stared at him, intently. "Sure. Head on out to the balcony. We'll join you in a sec."

****

Sam finished his description of the car bomb and shivered with an adrenaline spike. "You won't believe this," Sam continued, "but I swear, there was a woman there. Yeah, I know the police said it was a hallucination. I know what I saw."

Von shook his head. "You know, I've seen guys with battlefield hallucinations from trauma. That's not so unusual…"

Jake set his hands at his hips, thumbs in the belt loops. "What did she look like?"

"Who?" Sam asked distractedly.

"The girl with the broken leg. What did she look like?"

"Oh. Bright red hair. More than anything, she reminded me of a kid from an 80s movie. You know, like Madonna, those little lacy gloves with the fingertips cut out. Little clips in her hair…"

Jake nodded. "I get the picture." He knew immediately it was Red who somehow intervened to save Sam. This was the last of Desmond's premonitions. *The danger of fire is the destruction of evidence.* Jake also knew this was Asher exercising his darkest fantasies. Jake turned to Von. "I may be over-cautious, but humor me…"

"You're the boss. What you say goes."

"I want at least one guard on Cricket all the time until Asher is behind bars. Tonight is a party, so let's make sure it's not obvious. Have them wear something festive. There are enough of us to make it look like we're all simply socializing. Just everyone circulate and have a good time. The important thing is, she's never more than an arm's length from a bodyguard."

"Sure. We can do that. Tomorrow I'll have the dogs brought over too."

"Okay. That's great." The premonition of danger didn't leave Jake's heart.

****

An hour before the official start time, Paul and Sandy arrived with a box of Bluetooth speakers and a playlist from Boot Scootin' Boogie to Led Zeppelin.

"Where do you want these speakers set?" Paul asked as Jake hugged Sandy hello.

"How many speakers did you bring?" Jake nodded his head at the box of palm-sized Bose wireless speakers.

"Just six, but this house has a few levels, I'll scatter them around." Single-mindedly, Paul left Jake and set speakers around the two grills and outdoor seating areas.

Sandy's gaze swept the wide-open floor plan that included the amazing view of Richardson Bay and the Golden Gate Bridge. "You've come a long way from our spare room. What, you don't like sharing a bathroom?" She playfully punched Jake's arm.

"Hey, I still share a bathroom. It's a huge bathroom, but we share."

Sandy put her fingers in her ears, "I don't want to hear about that."

"You and Paul are a big part of my success in rescuing Cricket. She has a warm spot in her heart for you two."

Cricket appeared from the hall, "Are you talking about me?"

Jake swept his arm around her shoulder. "Speak of the devil."

"Paul has the speakers in place; he's about to start the music." Cricket nestled into his embrace.

Jake was accustomed to seeing her aura in various joyous shades of violet, blue and green, but tonight a cloud of black encroached upon her. Not actually touching her aura but coming close. He knew it foretold Asher's intentions. He strained to hold onto his party persona.

"That dress certainly shows off the healthy roses in your cheeks. You stay right beside me all night so that I can appreciate you."

Cricket pecked a quick kiss on his lips and nodded to Sandy. "Have you ever seen such a hopeless romantic?"

Sandy's gaze traveled from Cricket to Jake and nodded silently. "I'm going to check out the view and grab an Arnold Palmer." Jake felt her gaze as she left. It was that suspect look over her shoulder that told him; she was aware of his concern.

****

The appetizers lay on trays on the kitchen island; the cooks prepared the vegan and carnivorous foods on separate trays side by side. Then, it was time for Cricket and Jake to answer the ringing doorbell.

The security staff/valets vetted every guest. They cheerfully intermingled in the crowd, dressed in cowboy gear for the bar-b-que theme.

****

Joan Carroll hugged Jake and Cricket together. "Brian's doing the heavy lifting tonight." She nodded to her boyfriend sagging under the weight of pushing a dolly with a five-foot bronze garden statue. "We brought you an angel as if you need another one."

Brian sighed, "Have you got someplace I can put this for right now? This thing weighs a ton!" He balanced the handle to keep his grip.

Cricket hugged Joan in thanks, "Von, can you take… ooh, this is Michael, the archangel, to the deck for the evening?"

Von, six foot four and muscled to match, accepted the dolly like a stack of books. "I'll place it on the bottom deck so you can see it from above."

****

The thirty or so people who were personal friends, police, medical personnel, Coast Guard, and attorneys sat in small groups on the deck under the stars. As the catering staff cleared away empty plates, another team rolled around a dessert cart and encouraged people to choose a decadent treat.

Jake waited until the sounds of oohs and awes over the desserts waned and then stood. "None of this would have been possible without your teamwork." He held a bottle of Dos Equis up in a toast. "That includes my helpers from the spirit world. I'll bet each of you has a particular story to tell about your connection to us. As you finish your dessert, Cricket would love to hear the stories."

Paul lowered the music as people stood and recounted a humorous or touching moment.

Chapter 32

A small fishing boat bobbed in Richardson Bay; the engine cut so Asher could catch the sounds carried on the evening breeze. When the music was almost imperceptible, people passed a microphone to tell stories. They identified themselves first. *Fantastic, better to make my list.* Then they dragged on with some insipid story of their part in Cricket's rescue. Asher thumbed names into a memo app on his cell phone.

These are the sappiest tales ever. How they rescued my wife from her just rewards. Great, the retired cop has arrived on his boat. I'll deal with him at the marina.

****

Jake shivered underneath the warm night sky. It was more warning than temperature. His gaze swept repeatedly over the men in bright plaid western shirts. He counted all evening, three in blue plaid, three in red plaid. Von and his second in command wore brown plaid. To Jake, as the smell of charcoal and grilled food dissipated, he only caught the scent of his acrid sweat.

The auras of their guests amazingly displayed a rainbow of cheer. If he looked just at them, it was a haze of happiness. Then there was Cricket, seated beside him with that nagging black cloud inching toward her. *It seemed too early to disperse the party, but he always had her health to consider and people will graciously go home if the guest of honor excuses herself, right?*

Barry took the microphone. "After thirty years with the San Francisco Police Department, I can say I've never dealt with someone like Jake." A roll of light laughter greeted his words. He drew in a deep breath and grinned. "I'm kind of an old hippy, but the things Jake told me made me think he was trippin'. I thought I was going to collect some gas money, ride him over to an island and back and be done. Man, this was a helluva way to end my career. Cricket, you two have quite a story to tell your grandkids." He raised his beer bottle, "I'm proud to be a part of that story."

****

Cricket stood before her vanity mirror and removed her earrings. "I think everyone had a great time. What an odd mix of people. I love them all." She watched Jake's nervous movements as he walked from window to window. She turned and watched him leave the bedroom. "Where ya going?"

"Just checking all points of entry."

"Isn't that Von's job?"

"Can't hurt to check twice. We've got a man out front; we have the security system; I want to double-check them."

"When the dogs are delivered tomorrow, I can't wait for you to do a 'Vulcan mind-meld' with them." She laughed. "You have to show me how. Maybe we can get Sparkle potty trained in a hurry."

"You better hope we bought enough puddle pads for little Sparkle." He joked, and then Jake's demeanor darkened. "If anything goes awry, I want you in that closet immediately." He pointed to the newly installed safe room hidden in the back wall of the closet. "Don't come out of that safe room until you hear Von's or my voice."

Cricket nodded solemnly. "We've been over this before, Jake, I understand."

****

The house went to sleep. Cricket slumbered peacefully at his side, but Jake lay tense, awake and watchful. Every ship horn startled him; every creak of the tall frame home shook him. He was at odds to explain the night's noises. He stared out the window at the starlight. The one boat he'd seen earlier was gone. *Good. One less thing to worry about.*

****

At moonset, one-twenty-one in the morning, Asher listened to the sounds of silence. The homes along the shore were dark; only the garden lighting showed the path he'd take to enter *his* house. *Did the boy genius my wife took in find the hatch in the sub-basement? Probably not. The last time I was there, I covered it with a tarp and a gallon of paint.*

Drifting peacefully with a trolling motor, Asher tied his stolen Jon boat to the dock two doors down. Wading through a foot or two of water was annoying, but not as irritating as that gadfly Jake King. He'd like to crush that boy like a bug. Every few feet, Asher compulsively checked for the knife at his waist. *Blades are silent; they are up close and personal. Explosions are iffy, didn't this afternoon prove that? Guns are loud and leave a residue. Cricket's new-age boy-toy will be simple to eliminate no matter what route I take. Let's see how he likes knives.*

When Asher pulled himself up to the lower deck, he startled at the shadow of a winged man. *What the hell is this? Art? Please!* He circled the five-foot statue and shook his head. *Is this the way Cricket's boy-toy sees himself? An avenging angel, sword ready to defend her?* With a dismissive shake of his head, he crept toward the underside of the upper deck. Lifting the basement access panel, he shoved the paint can and tarp aside and pulled up into the sub-basement. He sharpened his hearing for alarms. *Nothing.* Using his penlight, he took the stairs to the basement door. He wiggled the doorknob, locked. He shone the light through the crevice and saw the door was armed with a sensor. *Dammit. I'm going to have to use the upper deck and break through a glass door.* He checked his waist for the industrial glass cutter. *Fine, score one for you.*

He turned to the door leading to the deck. *Idiots! They didn't put a sensor on this door. They might as well have welcomed me in.* Standing on his deck's second level, the night air felt heavy. The fog gathered like dark felt. Asher crept to the railing to assess points of entry.

"You don't belong here." A young woman looked up from a book.

Who the hell reads in the dark? Asher's paranoia vibrated, and he clung to the railing. "Who the hell are you?" he whispered, his throat closing on his words. The red-headed girl chuckled softly. She wore some getup leftover from the western-themed party. She pushed her linen blouse's neckline back on her shoulder and stood, adjusting her western skirt. "What are you supposed to be, Marshal Dillon's saloon girl?"

The lady strolled to the railing but kept her distance from him. "Well, you're right smart. At one time, I was. But I've been so many things to so many people."

In front of him, she morphed into the college freshman he'd strangled in a car on lover's lane almost ten years ago. *The bitch said I raped her. I couldn't have that.* Her visage was decayed and damning. Asher wiped his eyes. "Was it good for you too, Asher Winslow Parks? I was dead before you came. Nice technique, asshole."

"You're dead; you were nothing… less than nothing…"

The college freshman snapped her fingers, "And yet, I'm here! You've been a bad boy, Asher."

Asher charged the woman, knife out, slashing. "You're not real. I don't believe in ghosts." The figure evaporated, and Asher stood fighting for breath.

He heard his mother's voice. "You don't have to believe in ghosts, dear. We believe in you." His mother stood at the other end of the deck with her usual imperious posture. "I should have seen your vile acts coming. Better yet, I should have drowned you in the bathtub when you were a toddler. You were a nasty little snot even back then."

Asher kept his distance and looked at her through his eyelashes, his head dropped. He ran his thumb over his knife's blade. "Gee, I wonder where I got that from? Your whole side of the family was crazy."

His mother's figure shimmered in the moonlight, and Kathy Nielson appeared in her place. "What about me, Asher? We were never anything but kind to you."

Asher stalked toward his mother in law. "You and that pompous husband of yours never let me forget my degree was in business and not in software. I wasn't fit to run your company.

Kathy shook her head. "Cricket is far better off without you."

Asher charged her and hit the railing, nearly knocking the breath out of him. He held the sturdy railing and choked in damp air. He dared a look over his shoulder, and he was alone.

Asher straightened his shirt in his trousers and rechecked for his knife and glasscutter. Gathering his wits, when he raised his head, he saw a debilitated Cricket, wearing a hospital gown, tubes and wires hanging by her side. "You know, what you did to me is unleashing the wrath of the universe. But I have to give it to you. Once I knew how to navigate the astral plane, Jake was there to save me."

Asher ground his jaw. "That's all bullshit. You and your airy-fairy ideas of the universe. Meditate on this." He raised his knife and menaced Cricket.

He bounced off the fully formed corporeal being. The first woman, the gayly dressed redhead returned and threw up her hands.

As energy radiated from her, her previously sweet and sensual face grew grotesque and malevolent. "I died a horrible death at the hands of someone just like you. I've waited for this night for a hundred years." She pointed in the direction of Cricket's bedroom. "My sole task has been to prevent another woman from dying as I did."

Asher resisted the force field, gouging and punching in different directions, attempting to overtake the figure. Red released the ghostly shields, and with supernatural strength, yanked his knife from his hand and the glass cutter from his belt. He dropped back and gaped as she threw the items toward the bay.

Her visage softened, he smelled roses and violets. Before him, she was the epitome of feminine western beauty. Her copper locks curled around creamy white shoulders. Her corset encased dove-pale breasts. Her green eyes sparkled invitingly. When she cocked a hip and held up one side of her silky rustling skirt, Asher was bedeviled. When she crooked a finger at him, he dared tentative steps toward a goddess.

Red's petite physique belied her might when she threw her arms around his waist and pressed alluringly into him. Asher felt nothing but soft skin and a welcoming caress. His desire immediately awoke, and he grabbed her with both arms, burying his face in her neck.

The roses and violets faded into the scent of tobacco and campfires. The goddess in his arms became skeletal and overpowered him. Their gazes locked as her sweet eyes became cadaverous. He wrestled to break her hold, and the stench of death erupted from her parched lips.

"It's just a shame they wasted so much money on lawmen; all they had to do was ask me to take out the rubbish." Asher's gut churned as he felt his insides liquefy. Her wasted hand covered his mouth. "What I wouldn't give to have a night with you and get back for every woman you have ever hurt."

Asher's lungs burned in the attempt to scream.

"But I'm workin' my way to heaven, and that wouldn't be charitable."

Asher's feet attempted to kick and dispel the demon. She grabbed tighter, threatening to force the air out of his lungs.

"I'll see you in Hell." Were the only words he could sputter as she levitated both of them as if weightless. Within a swirl of effervescent air, they floated.

"Oh, honey, you're going there by yourself…" for an instant they hovered over the bronze St. Michael, his wings unfurled, his fist raised with his sword aimed downward to the demon under his foot.

Asher choked out, "Damn you." The statue's sword flamed. Red gathered the altitude to truly get her job done and then released him. For a moment, he flailed in the air as if he might fly. Then, with an anticlimactic thud, Asher's body dropped, impaled through his chest by the crest of a wing and St. Michael's fist.

"Oops!"

Chapter 33

Jake bolted upright in bed. Between the starlight and the moon, he clearly saw the deck. Silently leaving his bed, he tiptoed to stand in front of his ghostly friend, Red.

"I heard you protected Sam today."

Red fingered her beaded necklace and shrugged. "It was nothing; you'd have done it if you could."

"You look incredible, I've never seen you this fully formed. What's up?"

Red faux grimaced with a nod of her head. "I wouldn't say what's up. I'd say, what's down, over there." Red walked to the railing and pointed to Asher, dead on the statue. Jake dashed down the stairs. Red sauntered behind him.

"What did you do?" Jake circled the statue and Asher's unmoving body.

"He came after me. Just like men do. Like he always did. I was the hand of God, here to protect you and Cricket."

Jake dropped to his knees and rubbed his fists in his eyes. "I don't know how I slept through this… I should have intercepted him." Jake rose and began pacing the deck, running his hands through his dark hair.

"Jake, it's alright. This was meant to be. I can go now." Red approached him and held out a ghostly hand. "Can't you see, I'm evaporating before your eyes. Pretty soon, I'll be nothing but a memory."

Jake turned toward the sound of heavenly singing in the sky over the bay. "Here comes the light for you, Red. I guess I'll see you when it's my time."

Red, encompassed by the exquisite iridescent light, smiled radiantly. "We'll have a party, Jake." And she was gone.

Jake stared at the gruesome reality of Asher impaled. Quietly, he walked to the front door and summoned the guard. "We need to call the police." He gestured toward the lower deck.

The guard looked over the railing. "Holy shit, what the hell happened?"

Jake shook his head. "I guess he slipped, trying to climb up. I heard a thud, and this is what I found."

The guard had his phone in hand dialing 911.

Epilogue

Sedona Arizona, Six Months Later

Cricket sipped her tea in the shade of the lanai overlooking the Airport Mesa area of West Sedona. The fragrant vines and plants potted on the patio made the afternoons especially relaxing. The never-ending majesty of colorful striations within towering rocks fascinated Cricket hourly. It was like Diamond Head in Hawaii; the clouds played games revealing the rock's different colors. Jewel colored hummingbirds gathered at her feeders.

Cricket could tell the time of day by the prop planes landing and taking off nearby. The sacred stillness was what she had been seeking all her life. Red's diary, a leather book from over one hundred years ago, sat open in her lap. She felt a little guilty. She should be working on her note's for their Healing Center, but lately, she got tired in the afternoons.

When the lazy hawk circled above, it sounded off as it did every day about this time. "Look, look at me. I can fly," the hawk seemed to say.

Cricket placed the ribbon between the sturdy pages of the diary and winked at the bird. "I can, too."

The blindingly clear blue sky, the ochre of the rocks and the evergreen of the shrubs never dimmed in their startling beauty. She felt at home within this peaceful community. It was nothing less than a miracle that she was here now.

She heard Jake open the kitchen door and drop his keys in the brass bowl on the counter. His voice warmed their home as he greeted their fur babies. The three dogs welcomed him with friendly barks, and wagging tales, Sparkle's bark higher and lighter than her parents. As ferocious as they could be, they were merely happy dogs now. The kitten in her lap raised her head, yawned with a flick of her tiny pink tongue, and tucked her head back down. *Can it be any more perfect?* "I'm out back." She called quietly, trying not to disturb the kitten's rest.

Jake strolled to the lanai and dropped a kiss on top of her head. "You're not working on our project?"

Cricket winced, and her shoulder rose. "It's my kitty break."

"When does our print manager expect you to turn in your first draft?" He found his usual seat opposite her and toed off his shoes.

Cricket rolled her eyes. "They want the first draft within fourteen days."

Jake tilted his head back to catch the sun's rays, eyes closed, he chuckled. "How close are you?"

She held up her forefinger and thumb, "About this far."

He sat up immediately. He held both hands out at shoulder width. "And don't you need to be about this far?"

She giggled. "Slave-driver. I need more photos."

He reached for her hand.

She squeezed his fingers and shook her head. "Jake, I'm devouring the peace here. What a change in living. I love you so much."

He patted her hand and pointed two fingers at her, "Back atcha, damn right." He slid his sunglasses back down and resumed his sunbathing.

"How's the construction going on the center? Are the mineral and mud baths working yet?"

"Well, let's see. Everything is taking twice as long as the contractor promised, and we're being robbed blind. So, standard, I guess.

"I got an email from Barry; his group is riding along the Olympic Peninsula. He sends his best. He wants to know his odds with a certain blonde on the trip."

Cricket slid down her sunglasses. "Excuse me? There's a lot of blondes out there."

"I told him to make a move, be a gentleman, but make a move."

Cricket extended her hand to Jake and their fingers laced. "I'm glad you made your move."

He kissed the back of her hand and grinned his best crooked smile. "I was in the studio this morning recording some meditations. One was the Atlantis Healing Center. Want to hear it?"

"Okay, sure. Let's listen. See if it will put me under."

"As a meditation leader, if it doesn't, I need to rethink my career." Jake pulled out his phone and played his audio recording. "Assume a comfortable position. Let your body begin to relax.

Focus on your breathing; in to the count of three, out to the count of three…"

At first, Jake observed Cricket's breathing and body as she settled into the meditation. Slowly he found himself going under as well. It was unusual for two people to come together in the same meditation scenario, but she and Jake had done it from the beginning.

****

Jake found himself, side by side with Cricket in an area of lower desert. The terrain was more scrub brush than evergreens. The air was hotter and dustier. *Could we be in Cottonwood? Jerome?* Wherever they were, the setting was bleak.

A ramshackle clapboard house stood on a dirt lot. A junker of a car dominated the yard. Beside the car, a little girl about six years old wearing clothes two sizes too small cried. She clutched a ragged doll as dirty as she was.

Cricket bent down to her. "Hi, sweetie. Your dolly looks sad." The child nodded, rocking in her crouch. Her toenails displayed chipped and grown out bright pink nail polish. Her fingernails were chewed to the quick. "What's she sad about?"

"Her mommy won't wake up."

Jake's gaze met Cricket's as they crouched to the child. He forced a comforting smile. "Is mommy in the house?"

"Yes." Eyes swimming tears met his. Steeling himself, Jake headed for the front door, noting the sagging address plaque and a notice of eviction nailed to the faded door. He opened it, went in, and was greeted by the odor of cigarette smoke, rotting food, and urine.

A young mother in spirit form, wearing torn yoga pants and a crop top stumbled out of the bedroom to confront him. "What are you doing in my house?"

"You know your little girl is outside crying?"

"Why, what did you do to her?" The woman lifted an impudent chin.

"She's crying because she can't wake you up. Do you mean to leave her motherless?"

"Maybe she'd be better off without me." The woman stared out the window and saw Cricket. "That lady, she'd be a better mother than I've been. After tomorrow, we won't have a home."

"We'll look after your little girl, but it would be infinitely better if you come back into your body and seek treatment. We could help you."

"Why would you do that? I don't have anything to give you."

"You don't know what you might give the world until you try. You've already given the world a gifted child. She called us here. One in a million can do that."

Tears welled in the mother's haunted eyes. She folded her arms across her chest and shivered, her spirit paling as they spoke.

"I'm going to call someone, and we will meet you at the Cottonwood hospital. Your daughter can stay with us while you recuperate."

"Yeah, okay…" her voice trailed off.

"What's your name, and what's hers?" He nodded toward the yard.

"I'm Frankie. Her name is Harper." She smiled weakly, and her spirit drifted lackadaisically back into her body.

****

Jake snapped into consciousness and dialed 911. He remembered the address of the house listed on the eviction notice, the dangling home address plaque. He sent the paramedics racing toward the mother and child. Within minutes, Cricket was beside him, and they were en route to the Cottonwood Hospital.

Will this be our life now? Will souls in trouble forever reach out to us? We have the resources to help and to what better use could they be put?

They broke all speed limits getting to the hospital and Jake loped up to the ER desk, Cricket close on his heels. "Excuse me; a young woman was brought in…"

"Are you the uncle?" The clerk nodded at the lost looking six-year-old sitting with her behind the counter. "Harper said her uncle and aunt were coming."

Jake gaped, and Cricket stepped into the breach. "Yes, that's us. Harper, come here, honey."

The little girl hopped off the chair and ran to embrace Cricket's hips. Jake regained his tongue. "How's her mom?"

"Is Ms. Barnes, your wife's sister, or your sister?"

Jake looked around, "She's my sister, Barnes is her married name."

"Where is Mister Barnes?"

Jake shrugged noncommittally. "How is she? Is she going to make it?"

The clerk smiled kindly. "I'm sure the doctor will be out to speak with you when he can. The cafeteria is on the third floor if you want to keep your niece busy."

"Could you please text me if we're not here when the doctor comes out?" Jake wrote his number on a sticky note.

Harper refused to leave Cricket's side. "Are you hungry, honey?" Harper whined and shook her head. "We're going to get milkshakes, what's your favorite flavor?"

"Chocolate." That word brought a grin to the child's dirty face.

****

Once they were assured Frankie Barnes was in serious condition but expected to survive, they decided to take Harper to their home. Jake looked in the rearview mirror at Harper with her milkshake, "Do you like bubble baths?" Harper nodded without taking her lips off the straw. "Why don't we stop at the store and you can get your favorite bubble bath and some pajamas. You like stuffed toys?"

Harper shook her head and held up her dolly. "Dolly needs a dress."

When they reached the strip mall, Jake and Cricket shielded the child from curious stares. Cricket took her into a dressing room while Jake plucked things off the rack for their review. As Jake slipped the curtain back, he smiled at the sight of Harper, resting her cheek against Cricket's lower abdomen. With a gentle pat, the child smiled up at the two of them.

"I can't wait to meet him…"

Cricket's jaw dropped. "Him?" Her gaze met Jake's.

****

Once peace fell over their home, Jake slid the pregnancy test out of the bag. "It says first morning's urine, but I bought two, cause I'm impatient."

Cricket smirked as she left him to use the test. A few moments later, she walked out to the lanai. Jake stood under the wide indigo blanket of twinkling stars. She held out the stick. "A plus sign means pregnant a minus line means not pregnant."

Jake's eyes grew wide. "That's the boldest plus sign I've ever seen." He threw his arms around Cricket, and their joy bubbled between them. Jake looked over the mountainous vista toward heaven "You have something to do with this, Grampa Art?"

A shooting star swept across the velvet sky. Cricket winked, "Is that an answer?"

Jake grinned down at her. "He just said, see you soon, Mom and Dad."

The End

Thank you for reading our book. If you enjoyed our story, the greatest gift you can give us is a simple review wherever you bought the book, at BookBub, GoodReads, or other book websites.

We look forward to meeting you at one of the many Author/Reader events listed on our Facebook page.

Appetite for Blood, Prequel to the Blood Trilogy

A revolution is roaring into the 1920s! Vampires, who previously killed to feed, now thrill to feed.

The revolution is led by a four-hundred-year-old vampire, Rick Hiatt, and his newly turned ward, Matt Brenner. This is not the first time Rick has encountered the brutal treachery of the Moreau family of vampires, but he and Matt seek to make it the last.

Los Angelinos mortal and immortal are under attack by the entitled, remorseless Moreaus. Dragon-shifter Adam Lachlan and seductresses Venus and Luna, team up with Rick and Matt to put an end to the siege. Brute strength won't take these hellions down, but they might be hoodwinked into exposing themselves.

Read about the origins of the fast friendship between Matt, Rick, and Adam, and see how their BDSM empire grew from humble beginnings to an international conglomerate.

Blood Rising, Book One of the Blood Trilogy

Drop-dead gorgeous alive; Matt Brenner has never lacked for feminine attention. Undead, he's even more potent. Immortality would be stellar if only he accepted his life as a vampire. Matt and fellow vamp Richard Hiatt created a BDSM empire catering to Vampire/Doms and willing donor/subs who trade sexual ecstasy for blood. The clubs have made Matt's existence manageable, if uninspired.

Inspiration comes in the form of Catherine Temple.

Matt's made it a rule not to get emotionally involved with human women, and he sticks to it. Cat is the woman who can entice him to break all the rules. When Matt is introduced to a controversial drug that allows him a human lifetime with Cat, it's too exquisite to resist.

Powerful elements of the vampire nation are against it, and though Matt tries to protect Cat, love must be stronger than death.

Blood Emerald, Book Two of the Blood Trilogy

SDV (Single Dom Vampire) unknowingly ISO compassionate, sincere, spontaneous SMW (Single Mortal Woman). Extra points for patience, brains, and beauty. Handsome, powerful, Rick Hiatt has managed romance and sex within the roles of Dom/sub relationships for five hundred years. What if there is something more? What if the delicious Anna Curley, shielded from the world of dark sex games, can show him?

Rick returns to the helm of his international BDSM Empire after confronting a disaster within his vampire Family. His nemesis, Veronique Moreau, could destroy the fragile veil between the Vamp/Mortal worlds, leaving vampires exposed. He meets Anna, a guileless young woman with enough savvy to see trouble coming in the form of a vampire hunter.

Their worlds collide. Swept into the dangers of preternatural conflict, Rick and Anna experience exquisite passion, and heart-stopping peril. Is love enough? They could lose their lives as well as their hearts.

Blood Dragon, Book Three of the Blood Trilogy

Adam Lachlan, a tall drink of scrumptious masculinity, has been exiled from his dragon-shifter clan for the past two hundred years. His bad-boy charm has been harnessed to succeed as a Master Dom in the mortal world. He's spent decades isolating himself emotionally.

Willow Greer is beautiful, intelligent, and charming. Men have pursued her, but she's flown from them all. Willow has a secret burden. Adopted in infancy and having no explanation for shifting into a Pegasus at puberty, she's cloistered herself romantically. Without knowing the full truth of her nature, how can she commit to love?

When Adam's fire meets Willow's short fuse, flirtation is on! At the onset, secrets are guarded, but once their true selves are revealed, the complications begin. Can they overcome the problems of romance between different shifter species? Will they drop their emotional baggage and risk love's bondage?

Blood Fugue, Tales from the Gaoler, Book One
Fugue: [fyoog] noun
Psychiatry. A period during which a person suffers from loss of memory and often begins a new life.
You think your memory stinks?
Meet Harry VanAlt. An apex predator with fading memories of mortal life. Along with his memories, his exalted vampiric powers have faded to vampire-lite. Great taste, less exciting.

Along comes Dr. Lizbet Mitchell, a police profiler who has not yet opened the right door on her future. Thirty-four and questioning, when Harry rescues her from a rogue vampire, she invites him into her button downed life.

Her fascination meets his reticence as flashes and images from some other life intrude on his own.

A 16th-century ceremony reveals Harry's memories and unlocks his powers.

When Lizbet challenges Harry, they take steps toward a new and powerful immortality. Henry has two flesh and blood details to reconcile.

Harry closes the door on 1951 and settles a score.
#ParanormalRomance

Roman's Revenge, Roman's Adventures, Book 1
Jax Roman is the image of courage, nobility, and strength. A clever mind and agile body propelled Roman to the head of his SEAL class.

Handsome and disarming, Jax is in charge of his world, vertical and horizontal. Now, at the pinnacle of his game, he leads his own team until…the Lobos Cartel, the worst Jax has ever fought, sets out to eliminate him.

Lovely and compassionate, Dr. Kameo Alana meets Jax in his most desperate hour. Her family has borne the cartel's punishment.

Without Kameo, Jax would not be free to topple the depraved cartel.

Kameo is more than a balm for his pain. Together they sizzle white-hot.

Jax's mission for a 'happily ever after' with Kameo is an exercise in *'taking no prisoners', SEAL style.*

Roman's Rules, Roman's Adventures, Book 2

A complicated situation...

Kirk Roman knows he is the reason his relationship with Jordan Perry has never gotten to first base. His insecurity has been an ongoing barrier between them — until the day a sultry woman with her eye on him makes him re-evaluate his feelings for Jordan.

Jordan Perry is a fighter — and she is a survivor. She thought being widowed at thirty-seven was the worst that could happen until her diagnosis seven years ago. Clean, cleared, but scarred from her battle with breast cancer, Jordan silently dreams of the one man who has kept her going — Kirk Roman.

Kirk's inner battle with his desire to date Jordan isn't only about his insecurities. Jordan is a friend and an employee — two things he doesn't want to jeopardize. What he doesn't expect is the arrival of his estranged adult son and his wife.

The complications escalate when the sultry woman after him has a murderous past. Will all this kill his chance of finally telling Jordan how he really feels about her?

Will Roman's old rules work in this new situation?

Roman's Return, Roman's Adventures, Book 3

Conner

A young cowboy with his boots in the Texas dirt and his heart set on flying fighter jets, until love makes a course correction on a flight to meet his unknown father.

Skyler

An artist gifted beyond her years stands up for herself and wins a place at a prestigious art institute. A stalker shadows her path and drives her back to the last place she was happy.

Their Fate

Each had dreams tailoring their perfect futures. Will their long-held dreams nurture their love? Or, will the tolls of achieving their ambitions drive them apart?

Becoming Gabriel

Meet Gabriel Lee, if he were a young billionaire, his last few years would have earned him celebrity status. But, he's a mechanic in Baltimore's inner city. Past regrets haunt him. Can he ever win in a rigged system?

Opposites attract when Grace Lerner trades abusive privilege for freedom. Suddenly homeless, she meets Gabriel, and in their unlikely bond, they find soulmates come from the darndest places.

When Gabriel's ghosts endanger their joy, criminals cause a painful separation. Will their devotion deliver their happily ever after?

Arise, My Darling

Strangely gifted Jacob King finds Cricket Nielson in his meditations between worlds. Delightful Cricket is a woman trapped first by injury and then her husband's villainy. Captivated by her buoyant spirit, intrigued by their elusive meetings, Jake uses his psychic talents to locate this imprisoned beauty.

Their meetings on the astral plane reveal they have loved each other for eons. This newly reignited love calls Jake to draw on every spiritual resource at his disposal. He convinces sympathetic law enforcement professionals to hear him out as he discovers a series of murders and knows Cricket is next.

Will the forces of the universe unite Jake and Cricket before the insidious serial killer strikes again?

#MetaphysicalRomance

Where to follow Amber Anthony

All Author

BookBub

BookSprout

GoodReads

https://www.AmberAnthonyWrites.com

Adagio Teas, Custom Blends, tagged 'Amber Anthony'

Do you enjoy Tea? Check us out at Adagio Teas!

We have custom blended teas to correspond to each of our books. Purchasing these teas supports various charities Search under 'Blends', Keyword tagged Amber Anthony at Adagio.com.

Arise, My Darling This tea is creamy, nutty, tasty, and highlighted with dried cherries. Teas: Almond Oolong, Almond, Cream. Accented With Cherry & Marigold Flowers.

Constantly Cricket Nothing keeps Cricket Nielson from traveling, everywhere. Let her bring her flavor and spice to you! Black Tea, Natural Caramel Flavor, Natural Creme Flavor, Cocoa Nibs, Natural Chocolate Flavor & Natural Vanilla Flavor. Accented With Cocoa Nibs & Safflower.

Intuitive Lover This tea is as responsive as Jake King, get comfy with a nice steaming mug of your Intuitive Lover. Black Tea, Ginger, Peppermint, Cloves, Cardamom, Cinnamon, Natural Cinnamon Flavor, Cocoa Nibs & Natural Chocolate Flavor. Masala Chai, Chocolate Chai, Peppermint. Accented With Chocolate Chips.

Each tea purchase benefits a charity with a 5% donation.